HULL-DOWN FOR ACTION

HULL-DOWN FOR ACTION

By Armstrong Sperry

Illustrated by the Author

The Junior Literary Guild
and
Doubleday, Doran & Company, Inc.

Contents

HULL-DOWN FOR ACTION

CHAPTER 1 Four Adrift

ALREADY the brig *Island Queen* was hull-down on the
horizon and pulling away fast. One by one her square-
rigged topsails disappeared beyond the flawless rim of
the Pacific. Another moment and they would be lost to
sight forever. And four boys clinging to a raft, drifting
at whim of wind and current, strained after their vanishing ship with their hearts in their eyes. Cries swelled
in their throats, choking them, to die unuttered. No use
to cry out when only the empty sky could hear! They
were stunned by the conviction that with the disappearance of the brig's canvas their last hold upon certainty,
upon life even, was slipping away.

So swiftly had events telescoped that there had been

no time to think: they had reacted to automatic instinct. Now there would be plenty of time for thinking! Days, weeks of it—if they could hold out that long. And this actuality bore in upon each of them in all its terrifying implications.

No food. No water. No sail. Scudding before the wind, they were without means of controlling the drift or direction of their buoyant craft. In the unpredictable days and nights ahead there would be only their ingenuity, their tough young strength to pit against the might and power of the sea.

Suddenly the horizon was swept clear.

"There she goes, mates," cried Judd Anders bitterly. "The last we'll ever see of her!" And honest anger blazed in his eyes, dominating despair.

"We're all in the same boat!" Conk McCoy tried to wisecrack. His freckled, hard boy's face forced a grin. "I reckon this is curtains, pals. It's been nice knowin' you guys!" He laughed without mirth.

Young Ken Henderson—erstwhile ethnologist on field duty for a Chicago museum—seemed dazed by the inescapable fact that he was actually adrift on a raft in mid-Pacific. Destination unknown. Survival doubtful.

Nothing in all his academic experience in museums, classrooms, or libraries had prepared him for such a contingency. Behind horn-rimmed spectacles Ken's eyes peered out more bewildered than dismayed.

"I guess we were all a pack of gullible fools," he managed finally. "Still, that Jap's papers were okay when you signed him on, weren't they, Judd?"

"Water tight," the other grudged, and his eyes were chips of flint. "Haru Osaka, native American born in Hawaii. Steward for three years on the S.S. *Matsonia*. Sober, industrious, polite . . ." The boy recited the words in singsong, as a bitter lesson that had been drilled into his brain.

"Jeepers," agreed Conk McCoy, "he was polite enough—the grinnin' little ape."

"And industrious, you'll admit," added Ken ironically. "No grass grew under *his* feet. Just another Son of Nippon dreaming of the Greater East Asia Co-Prosperity Sphere."

"*Dreaming* of it?" Judd exploded. "Scheming, slaving for it, you mean."

And suddenly in a slackening of nervous tension the three of them were jabbering at once, as if against that empty immensity of sea and sky the sound of their own voices restored some measure of sanity and self-confidence.

Only the fourth member of the band remained silent. This was Terii, a Samoan whose vocabulary included few words of English. But so well had this bronze young giant come to understand his shipmates during the recent months aboard the *Island Queen* that he was able to follow much of their speech by the expressions on their faces. Now the native was listening intently, dark eyes grave with concern.

3

For the moment, in unspoken agreement, the boys shied away from acknowledging the fact that they had been set adrift to die in the loneliest of oceans. Instinctively they sought to conceal their fear behind casual words.

Judd was saying: "How long's it going to take America to realize that Japan staked out a claim to the Pacific thirty years ago?"

"What do you suppose Osaka meant," Ken demanded, "by saying that today would go down in history? What day is this, anyway?"

"December seventh, Professor," Judd mocked, "and the year is 1941, in case you've forgotten!"

"All days are alike in this part of the world. What's so different about the seventh?"

"Search me! But it's half a year, remember, since we sailed from New Zealand. A lot can happen in that time."

"And no radio to keep us posted," Conk supplied. "Heck, not even the comics! I wonder what Superman's been up to."

"Remember the day we sailed?" Ken was asking. "Germany had just declared war on Russia. June twenty-second, wasn't it?"

"That's right. I wonder if Little Adolf knows he caught a bear by the tail?"

"Seems like a hundred years ago. . . ."

And with that, conversation petered and died. The gravity of the predicament in which they found themselves came driving home, silencing them, no longer to be denied. Now the only sounds were the wash of the sea against the raft, the hoarse croak of sea birds wheeling and planing against the sky: the red-tailed tropic bird, the frigate and the booby, the kingly albatross soaring across currents of the upper air. Already sharks were shadowing the raft, their knifelike dorsals patrolling in wary parallel. A light wind had set in from the northwest, driving the ocean swells before it. Without effort the raft slid down the back of one glassy hill, slowly mounted the incline of the next.

Imperceptibly the sea's color deepened with late afternoon; the sun in its westward stride cast a sheen that was a dust of gold across the entire visible sky, while a sense of loneliness almost palpable rose from the surface of the ocean.

"Where do we go from here, Skipper?" Ken's casual question voiced the thought stirring in the mind of each. "Not that we haven't plenty of time to decide . . ."

Judd's mouth set, his lean body tensed. "The first thing I need from you fellows is a vote of confidence," he told them. "I've been a blasted fool. It's my fault you're in this jam and it's up to me to pull you through. If I hadn't trusted that Jap and Einar Karlson——"

"Heck, forget it. Anyone would have done the same. Their papers were okay."

"That's no excuse," the other retorted stubbornly. "But what's done is done. We've got to pull together now. There'll be times when some one of us will have to make a final decision, and then——"

"That someone's *you!*" Conk's tone was positive. "You was skipper on the *Island Queen,* wasn't you? You're the only one of us can tell the Southern Cross from a shark's gill." He raised a wiry arm to proclaim: "I hereby nominate Judd Anders skipper of this ocean-going packet. All those in favor——"

"Aye!" Ken echoed with enthusiasm, while the giant Terii shouted a vigorous "*Ai*" which in his own tongue also meant yes.

The responsibility which this vote of confidence imposed upon Judd silenced him, humbled him too. And as well as the boy had come to understand his companions, he found himself searching them with fresh scrutiny, weighing them against the hazards that must be met and conquered. How long could they bear up under the merciless pressures of hunger and thirst, heat and cold, hope and despair? Which one would be the first to crack? With relief the boy dismissed Terii from his concern, secure in the belief that the young Polynesian had been conditioned by birth to survive at sea.

But there was Ken. Thin, bespectacled Ken was strong enough for any ordinary emergency perhaps. But he had been a landlubber all his life, living detached within a world of books and museums. Why, he couldn't even swim! And in spite of being twenty-odd he seemed only an irresponsible kid. Yet Ken never knew when he was licked. And to Judd this was vastly reassuring, for he was aware that untapped resources lie dormant within the kind of men whose minds never give up.

Judd's eye rested briefly on Conk McCoy's hundred and twenty-five pounds of whipcord and sinew. When Conk signed on as foremast hand six months before Judd had liked the tough, steady look which held neither challenge nor evasion. Trained in the school of hard knocks, Conk had battled and shifted for himself since childhood. Now, scarcely eighteen, he was as tough as hemp.

Yes, here was a fine crew! And Judd Anders felt a lift of gratitude; for he understood that while any one of them alone might survive for a long time, the four of them together could somehow manage to hold out even longer.

As for Judd himself, he'd lived too close to the hazards of the sea to harbor self-doubt in this emergency. Born in Tahiti, he had sailed his father's trading schooner throughout the atolls of the Dangerous Archipelago, learning navigation by that most practical of methods—sailing. At fourteen he'd been able to con a ship by the feel of the wind, to pick his way among the landmarks of the stars—an apprenticeship which now made him seem older than his nineteen years, investing him with the intangible quality of command.

He knew that he'd be needing all his knowledge of the winds' ways, of ocean currents and cloud formations—the myriad signs by which a practiced seafarer finds his way to land without aid of modern navigating instruments. Irrelevantly it occurred to the boy that the problems confronting him, adrift on a raft, were no more formidable than those which the first Polynesian navigators had been forced to solve. More than a thousand years before Columbus *they* had sailed the length and breadth of the Pacific, determining their position and course to nearest land without benefit of chronometer, sextant, or compass, guided only by sun and stars and their own sure instinct for the sea. And he, Judd Anders, could do the same! This conviction reached him like a challenge that brought his chin up.

"I'll do my best, mates," he promised. "But let's not kid ourselves. We're in for a tough pull and a long one. Whether we come through is anybody's guess. I know what our bearings were when we were put off the ship. And I know the Solomons are the nearest land. But eight hundred miles stretch between here and there. And," he concluded grimly, "we haven't much to work with."

"Let's take stock," Ken suggested. One after another he turned inside out the pockets of his bleached dungarees. "Empty!" His face dropped. "What a score! One shirt. One pants. One canvas belt complete with buckle. One pair of superspectacles. But not even a hat!"

"That Jap sure did a friskin' job," Conk admitted, searching his own pockets by squeezing them. He gave a wry grin. Cotton shorts and undershirt, the small gold cross suspended by a chain about his neck, remained his entire worldly possessions. "What a setup!"

Terii's gaudy red-and-white *pareu* was so scanty as to leave him practically mother-naked. His inseparable shark knife had been torn from the loop of cord that still dangled about his throat. The native spread his hands with silent eloquence. Terii had only his great strength to offer.

Meanwhile Judd, searching his own pockets without expectation, gave a sudden shrill whistle of amazement; for he withdrew a stub of pencil which had somehow been overlooked when his clothing was rifled. Here, he felt, was his first good break. "Boy, can I use this!" he exulted.

"Gonna write a book?" Conk queried sarcastically.

"A chart, screwball! *Now* we'll know where we're going!"

This first decision and the means to carry it out heartened Judd immeasurably. In awed silence the others looked on as their newly elected captain drew lines of latitude and longitude across one of the bleached planks decking over the central portion of the raft.

"This was our exact position when we left the ship," the boy explained, marking a circle on the improvised chart; to the southwest he formed a second circle. "And here's where we're headed, mates: the Solomon Islands. We're on our way!"

Conk grinned. "Looks like we're leavin' nothin' to go nowhere." But an undercurrent of admiration quickened the words and his eyes danced blue as the waters of Killarney. Conk had no understanding of the abstruse science of navigation but he was vastly impressed by it. "All you need is a little savvy," he crowed. "Leave it to the skipper! The firm's brains, that's what he is."

Roughly on the white planking Judd's pencil traced and bit deep: latitude and longitude. Greenwich date and time. Course and approximate distance to nearest land.

"There!" the boy finished with satisfaction. "Even if the sea washes off the record it's bitten into the wood."

Conk sighed: "Jeepers, if we'd only known when we built this raft we were gonna use it for a houseboat."

"You'd have had hot and cold running water, I suppose?" Ken snorted.

"I'd have had me a bunk with a mattress, and an awning to keep this blasted sun out of my eyes."

"How about a Crime Club library, just to pass the time?"

"I'd settle for fishin' tackle, Professor."

The boys themselves had constructed this raft weeks before on the coral shores of Vana Vana. Its purpose had been to transfer cases of rotted-out pearl shell to the hold of the *Island Queen*. Of native *purao* wood, the raft combined durability with corklike buoyancy. Poles a foot thick had been lashed together with lengths of coconut sennit to form a platform some eight by ten feet. Sennit such as Terii plaited was practically as strong as wire; it would endure until finally the sea should rot its fibers. A second thickness of poles had been lashed at right angles to the first, thus raising the platform a foot or more above the surface of the water. Down the center four planks had been fastened solidly with spikes—the only metal in the craft's construction.

"Let's rig life lines," Judd was saying. "We'd be up against it in a blow."

It was decided that the lashings along the center could be spared for this vital purpose.

"But how in heck are we goin' to cut 'em loose without a knife?" Conk wanted to know. "This stuff's like cable."

"Me cut," Terii volunteered. "You see!"

White teeth flashed, and instantly Judd understood; for often he had watched Polynesians rip open with their magnificent teeth a can of beef or beans. Mere sennit would present no obstacle to the Samoan.

The native flung himself flat; the others could see the working of his strong jaws, the muscles knotting his neck. Presently two lengths of cord severed cleanly, each some fifteen feet long, were produced by Terii, who gave a childlike laugh of triumph as he dashed the sweat from his face.

In no time the ropes were made fast: a grip and toehold for rough weather.

"Now," Judd urged, "if we can pry loose one of those planks we'll have a rudder. Otherwise we'll be sailing in circles."

Willingly they put their beef into the task. But the six-inch spikes had been hammered too securely into the purao, for in spite of the boys' combined effort the board refused to yield the fraction of an inch. They were forced to admit defeat for the time being.

Nursing bloody knuckles, Conk groaned: "We sure did a job, pals."

"We'll have another try at it in the morning," Judd promised him.

"I can hardly wait!"

Swiftly the sun had vanished, swallowed by the ocean. Afterglow, as always in these latitudes, was brief. The ensuing darkness seemed less an absence of light than an actual substance materializing from the surface of the water. A vastness of sea and sky reduced the raft and its burden to proportions scarcely larger in scale than the flecks of weed that drifted on the sea. Rank after rank the swells moved by, majestic and awe-inspiring, filling their hearts with a kind of wonder. Tropic birds and boobies, frigates and terns had vanished into some other dimension whose secret remained their own. With their passing the sense of loneliness increased, sharp and poignant. Only the sharks remained, tireless in vigil.

"Boy, what I could do to a ham sandwich," Conk was heard to mutter.

"How about a nice juicy tenderloin?" Ken suggested.

"Okay, pal. Let's go Dutch."

The brave and foolish banter expired. An awareness of danger, immediate and ominous, closed in upon them all, so that their tongues fell silent and they were grateful for night's concealing darkness which hid anxiety from one another. Off to port a first star glittered low on the horizon, malign and bright; dark water frothed across the raft, drenching its occupants.

"We'll set a watch." Judd's voice came terse. "You fellows get some sleep if you can. I'll stand first watch. Terii will relieve me. After that you, Ken. Then Conk."

"Aye, aye, sir."

While his shipmates stretched flat on the raft with hands and feet hooked into the life lines, Judd sat upright, arms locked about his knees. Staring ahead into darkness, he sought to reassure himself with solid facts: that this northwest wind was favorable, the sea not rough, the distance to known land a mathematical certainty. But disquieting fragments of all the stories he'd ever heard about men set adrift flickered across his mind like heat lightning in a sultry sky. Long ago his father had swapped such yarns with many an island trader; how little the listening boy of those years had suspected that a time would come when he too would find himself in such a situation! Like specters, those tales emerged now in all their gaunt detail: hunger . . . thirst . . . wind and storm . . . monsters fighting for survival in the unimagined depths of the sea . . .

Sternly the boy forced himself to concentrate upon the solid realities of ocean and sky. As the little raft went scudding across the swells his thoughts raced ahead of the following wind. So far luck was holding. Tomorrow he'd devise some means of controlling the raft's direction, work out a way to estimate its speed; otherwise his chart would be worthless. Why couldn't he rig a makeshift sea anchor out of his dungaree jacket? . . . Somehow he'd free that plank to make a rudder. . . . Thus his thoughts went racing.

Giant constellations, incredibly bright and near, were wheeling up the night sky. Eagerly the boy sought among them for the stars he'd need to steer by, while a part of his mind returned to those early Polynesians—more resourceful navigators than the Phoenicians or the Vikings. Which stars had *they* followed from Malaya to Tahiti, from Hawaii to New Zealand?

"But those fellows had sails and paddles," the boy mourned, "stores of food and water . . ."

Then he reminded himself that he was lucky to be alive. "It's only by the grace of God that little Jap didn't drill us all—just as he killed Sven Dineson."

And a pang shot through Judd at thought of the young Dane, first to suspect treachery aboard the *Island Queen* and to pay for loyalty with his life. For the hundredth time Judd Anders berated the blind folly which had betrayed him into trusting Einar Karlson. Yet, he reminded himself, that was what a first mate was signed for! Karlson had proven himself a crackerjack seaman; his papers were beyond reproach. Until today nothing in his behavior had been suspicious. As for Haru Osaka—Judd's fists knotted and he groaned aloud.

A caprice of wind slewed the raft around, spun it in a half circle. And the boy, catching his balance, was aware for the first time of bodily fatigue. So much had happened, and fast! At that moment the wind flung a bucket of spray against his body, drenching him, and he shivered with sudden cold. Stiffening, he willed himself to focus upon the patterns in the sky; but it seemed an interminable time until he heard Terii stirring, and he could say: "Take over, Terii."

"Ai, American." The big native slid to Judd's side, his presence solid and reassuring in the darkness. "The wind, it is holding?"

"Still holding."

"*Maitai!* That is good." The Samoan spoke in native tongue, voicing a thought which gave them both a deep concern. "American, the other two—they do not understand the ways of the sea as we do."

"True, Terii."

"Then we must think for them."

"That is right, my friend. You and I must carry them through."

"We can do that, American, no?"

"You bet we can!"

They gripped hands, a dark-skinned boy and a white one, pledging a pact which only death could bring to an end.

Fishing the pencil stub out of his pocket, Judd marked a single vertical stroke on the planking: *one day gone . . .*

Then at last the boy lay beside his companions. But weary though he was, sleep proved as elusive as a rainbow's end. Staring up at the black sky, his mind revolved in a squirrel cage of uncertainty and doubt, and at this dark moment confidence in his own ability seemed like sheerest impudence which surely the gods must punish. How could he hope to guide this cockleshell to land, across how many leagues of ocean, praying for rain to slake their thirst before the sun should have exacted its inexorable toll?

Higher and higher, swinging from east to west, the constellations climbed the ladder of the sky. And again the boy sought among them for some star to guide his course. Should it be Alphard, the "Lone Star," sailing through a deserted stretch of the heavens? Or Mata-Iki, Little Eyes, lodestar of the ancients? Then Judd discovered Scorpio, saw the blood-red fire of Antares flaming in the body's center; and to the southwest it pointed, straight and unwavering as the magnetized needle of some astral compass. Under its glittering extremity the Solomon Islands lay waiting.

"Old Scorpio," the boy thought drowsily, while his spirit lifted. "You were rising when I was born. You've always been my lucky star. What do you say? Will you show me the way now?"

Sleep stole upon him unawares, under the ancient flickering watch fires of his lucky star; while across the shadow world of the boy's mind there drifted a phantom procession of people and events: Sven Dineson lying dead on the deck of the *Island Queen* . . . Einar Karlson . . . and Haru Osaka smiling, always smiling

. . . What was Osaka saying? Ah yes . . . Judd could hear that voice now, silky, ingratiating. . . .

And suddenly it seemed that Judd Anders was back again in the cabin of the *Island Queen* where she rode at anchor on the deep lagoon, while Haru Osaka was murmuring: "Excuse, please, Captain. May I speak with you?"

CHAPTER II Suspicion

THE JAPANESE STEWARD'S voice never had sounded
more persuasive. "Excuse, please——"

Judd glanced up from a sheaf of charts to see Osaka
framed by the cabin doorway. The morning sun, only
an hour high, slanted obliquely through a porthole, sil-
houetting the short stocky figure. The little steward
looked immaculate as always in white jacket and ducks.
His black hair, jet and glossy as a crow's wing, grew
low on his forehead; and beneath a flat brow his eyes
slitted until they all but disappeared whenever the round
face stretched its ready smile. Undeniably an attractive
smile, brightened by extraordinarily white teeth.

"Well, Osaka?"

The Japanese hesitated, picking his way among words. "Excuse, please, sir . . . We will be leaving Vana Vana soon, no?" The smile vanished and the eyes reappeared, bead-black and bright.

Judd nodded absently, his thoughts elsewhere. He rolled up the charts and locked them in a chest which filled one corner of the cabin; the key he clipped on a ring fastened to his belt. There was method in this caution: Vana Vana, an atoll rich in pearls and black-lip shell, had first been sighted by a French surveying vessel in 1888 and erroneously charted some two hundred miles northwest of the Grand Coral Shoal—a devilish region of submerged reefs and treacherous currents. Only recently rediscovered,* the true position of the atoll remained the joint secret of Judd Anders and the New Zealand Colonial Government. At the moment when, logically, the island's existence would have been proclaimed to the world on the latest British Admiralty charts, England and her colonies had become embroiled in another war. Caution was the watchword.

Suddenly the insistence of the little steward's question struck through Judd's preoccupation; it was unlike Osaka to intrude. The boy's tone came short as he answered: "I'm planning to bring off the last of the shell this afternoon. But why are you asking?"

Embarrassment appeared to overcome the Japanese. He hung his head and dropped his eyes. "Five months the *Island Queen* has been here in Vana Vana," he mur-

*See *Lost Lagoon*.

mured. "When Osaka signed as steward he did not know it would be so long a time. *So* sorry, sir!"

"The expedition has taken longer than anticipated," the other acknowledged impatiently. "What's your hurry, Osaka? A sailor signs for the duration of a cruise!"

But the rebuke passed unheeded. The bright smile flashed again, and this time the little Japanese gave his familiar hissing chuckle. "I have what you call engagement, sir," he murmured blandly.

"Engagement!" Judd exploded. "How? Where?"

Osaka drew up to his full four feet eleven inches and with irreproachable dignity replied: "It is engagement for marriage, sir."

Now it was the other's turn to chuckle. "And the young lady is impatient—is that it?"

"That is true, Captain. Please, she waits in Honoruru. That is why I wish to know when we will be sailing."

Judd threw a glance at the calendar on his desk. "Today's the sixth. . . . With fair winds we'll raise Diamond Head by the twentieth. You can count on wedding bells in two weeks, Osaka."

"Excuse," the Japanese corrected quickly, "but today is December seventh!"

"Right you are!" And Judd tore off the outdated slip of paper, tossed it aside. In that second he surprised an inexplicable expression in Haru Osaka's eyes: a brightness, a glitter whose meaning he could not fathom. But it was as unexpected as a rumble of thunder on a fair day.

Instantly the black eyes were veiled as the wide smile flashed. With composure the little steward responded: "Thank you, sir. Now Osaka happy! Please, in two weeks he married."

At that moment Ken Henderson shouted from the corridor: "The canoe's ready, Skipper! Shake a leg!"

And with that Ken appeared in the doorway, looking like a gangling Boy Scout as he adjusted across his thin shoulders the canvas knapsack that contained hatchet, calipers and measuring tape, camera, notebooks, and pencils—those inseparable badges of his calling. Even though his ethnological research at Vana Vana had been completed, he would as soon have gone ashore without his indispensable spectacles as without his knapsack.

The Japanese backed away, still beaming. "Osaka very happy," he repeated. "*So* happy!" And with another hissing chuckle vanished.

"What's the little man so hopped up about?" Ken wanted to know.

"Says he's going to be married." Judd hesitated. "But . . ."

"He looked like the cat that swallowed the goldfish. Hey, if this is to be our last day let's get moving!"

On deck Sven Dineson stood waiting by the rope ladder, where an outrigger canoe rode restively under the brig's counter. The young Dane's expression was solemn, even melancholy; but to Judd there was nothing unusual in that fact. For Dineson seemed an ingrown sort of fellow who, since the beginning of the cruise, had held aloof from his fo'c'sle mates. Though an excellent sailor, he enjoyed little popularity with his fellows. Nor did he seem more congenial with his own countryman, the first mate, who now stepped forward and touched his cap respectfully to Judd.

"Any orders, Captain?" Einar Karlson was a well-built man in his mid-thirties, powerful about the shoulders and neck, trim about the waist. His close-clipped hair had been bleached by the tropic sun, and against his deeply tanned skin his eyes blazed like the icy waters of a fiord—eyes that could focus instantly to gimlet scrutiny. He looked competent and hard, able to take care of himself in any scrimmage. "Orders, Captain?" The voice was subtly grating, with the same Nordic accent that flavored the speech of Sven Dineson.

"See that the water casks are filled," Judd Anders told him. "Send men ashore for a boatload of coconuts— whatever fresh fruit they can find."

"Very good, sir."

"And shake out the canvas. I'm bringing back the last of the shell this afternoon and we'll weigh anchor with the ebb."

"*Ak*, so soon, Captain?" The mate expressed surprise.

"Not soon enough for Osaka," Judd returned, and could not have told what prompted him to add, "He has an engagement and doesn't want to be late."

Einar Karlson permitted himself his rare smile. "So he has yust told me! I vill see that all is ready. Ve cannot keep Nippon vaiting, sir."

If satire lurked in the mate's words, no reflection of it warmed the cold eyes; they remained entirely humorless.

As Sven Dineson dropped into the bow of the canoe that bobbed so impatiently alongside Einar Karlson flung his countryman a probing look. Then the mate lowered his voice, drew Judd Anders out of earshot. "May I ask your attention a minute more, sir?"

Surprised, Judd nodded. "Well?"

"It's about Dineson," the man began.

"What's the trouble?"

Karlson tapped his forehead significantly. "He's getting queer in the head, sir. In the fo'c'sle the men are saying at night he sees things—ghosts and such."

"He's always kept to himself." Judd hesitated. "But he's a good sailor——"

"It's not that! He imagines things that never happened. I thought I should varn you, sir, in case ve have to lock him up."

"I'm glad you told me but I hope it won't come to that. Dineson's a good man."

Without further explanation the mate swung about and disappeared down the companionway, leaving the boy mystified by the abruptness of his disclosure. Something about it didn't quite carry the ring of conviction and, irresolute, Judd sought the reason. But at that moment Ken shouted from the canoe: "Step on it, Skipper!"

"Coming!"

Terii, paddle in hand, had already taken his place on the stern thwart. Conk McCoy was amidships, baiting a villainous hook with a scrap of pork; for Conk looked forward eagerly to these shoreward excursions even though they meant the heavy work of loading shell. He was never so completely happy as when trailing a fishline. Sven Dineson sat huddled in the bow, absorbed in his thoughts.

Judd scrambled down the rope ladder, dropped into the stern. "Shove off, Terii!"

"Ai, American!"

The narrow craft swung clear of the brig's side as Judd hoisted the sail. Instantly the wind filled the canvas. The canoe raced on a long diagonal toward a spur of land jutting into the lagoon half a dozen miles away—the spot which had been chosen months before for rotting out the black-lip shell. But scarcely had a hundred yards been covered when Judd remembered the binoculars he'd left on the sea chest in his cabin. Without them he felt as handicapped as did Ken without his spectacles; and consequently the boy motioned to Terii to bring the canoe about and beat back to the ship—an operation that consumed some minutes.

Neither Karlson nor Osaka was in sight as the canoe slipped quietly under the brig's stern, but already fo'c'sle hands were aloft shaking the sails out of harbor gaskets; a smallboat swayed in the davits. Orders were being carried out as issued by the captain.

Judd sent Sven Dineson aboard to fetch the binoculars; and when at last the young Dane reappeared, glasses in hand, it was evident from his expression that he felt even gloomier than before. In fact so utterly downcast did he appear that Judd felt impelled to demand: "What's on your mind, Sven?"

But Dineson shook his head, maintaining moody silence as again he took his place in the bow. There he sat with shoulders hunched forward, presenting to the others a stubborn back. And for the first time it seemed to Judd that Karlson's statement was plausible, that Dineson *was* a bit touched in the head.

Once more Terii shoved clear of the brig as Judd ran up the sail. Under a freshening breeze the canoe leaped like an arrow released toward its mark, and for a few minutes Judd had his hands full. Presently a backward glance informed him that Einar Karlson had returned to deck, followed by Haru Osaka. Nothing strange in that. . . . But the two figures were standing by the rope ladder, staring after the canoe in what seemed to be attitudes of fixed concentration. And a sudden uncertainty welled up in Judd Anders—an unease that was a positive sensation and one he'd known before. It was like the sense of warning in the unreal greenish light of a day when a hurricane is making; like timing a delayed fuse of dynamite, knowing it was overdue and yet might still explode. And so seldom had that inner signal betrayed him that for a second he almost yielded to the impulse to return to his ship.

But a gust of wind demanded his attention as the canoe heeled over and raced on delicate balance for the distant shore. Easing the sheet a trifle, the boy again glanced back at the brig. This time he discovered that both figures at the rope ladder had disappeared. But the sense of unease lingered in his consciousness, disturbing as the hum of an unseen mosquito. For the first time Judd found himself wondering if unsuspected reefs had been lying hidden beneath the placid surface of the days.

Ken broke in on his preoccupation, pointing back toward the *Island Queen*. "Look at her, Judd! Isn't she a beauty?"

The brig lay glistening in the morning sun, immaculate against the rich background of lagoon and sky. But there was no need for Judd to voice his pride in the sturdy ship. How well he knew her points! He and Ken together had bought her from the Colonial Government with money from the sale of pearls they had discovered two years before at Vana Vana. And his thoughts skipped back over the time that had elapsed since he and Ken first beheld the fabulous atoll. For Judd, those two years had been spent at college on the mainland—another world from this tropical one he knew and loved. Ken, meanwhile, had been bogged down writing Polynesian monographs for his museum. Both of them had been marking time, for Vana Vana remained foremost in their hopes and plans.

Then, at the end of his sophomore year and with fine grades to his credit, Judd had been granted leave of absence for the first semester of the following term. An urgent wire to Chicago brought Ken on the run. They'd taken passage on the first ship leaving for New Zealand, where the *Island Queen* lay in dry dock. The bargain they'd driven with a harried Colonial Government would have done credit to a Philadelphia lawyer. Involved in a second World War, New Zealand granted permission to the boys to bring out the rare black-lip shell which lined the floor of Vana Vana's lagoon, to be sold on a fifty-fifty basis in the Hawaiian market. And as a concomitant to the enterprise, the Government extended the freedom of the atoll to Ken Henderson for ethnological research, waiving all claims on any discoveries.

Picking up a crew in wartime meant making shift with whatever men were available. With the exceptions of Sven Dineson, Conk McCoy, and Terii, Judd had signed half a dozen of the likeliest jailbirds he'd ever clapped an eye on. But his first mate was a stroke of good fortune: Einar Karlson's ship, the *Eklund*, had been torpedoed by a Nazi submarine; the Dane was seeking a berth for himself and for his mess boy, an American-born Japanese named Haru Osaka. Thus manned, on June 22, 1941, the *Island Queen* had pointed her nose toward the Grand Coral Shoal some-where between the Ellice and Gilbert Island groups, seeking an atoll whose exact bearings were locked in the sea chest in Judd Anders' cabin.

Though the cruise had proved uneventful, five months at Vana Vana seemed to pass with the speed of light. Even the thought of fat profits from tons of valuable shell stowed in the brig's hold failed to rec-oncile the boys to the fact that soon they must return to the humdrum grind of college and museum.

Thrusting aside that unwelcome thought, Judd de-termined to enjoy this last day to the full. With the sun beating hot upon his shoulders, a tropic sky vaulting overhead, he knew that this island world was where he belonged. Fervently he vowed that after he graduated he'd head for Tahiti like a homing pigeon, there to settle down on the coconut plantation which had be-longed to his parents, now dead. Cities would never know him again! He'd recapture that fine free life he'd led as a boy, sailing the *Island Queen* through the atolls of the Dangerous Archipelago. And Ken, the old fossil hunter, could go along too. What more could any fel-low ask?

Judd hauled the sheet tighter, spray leaped back from the prow. There was a surge and lift to the slim craft's motion like the take-off of a plane. Flying fishes broke water, their flight a shimmering arc brief-lived in the sun, while porpoises sped after them, so close at hand that the sound of their breathing was clearly audible.

Suspicion

Across the paler green of shallow water the canoe flashed, over gardens of unimaginable wonder, where fishes gleamed and flicked through branching staghorn corals, where sea grasses swayed in lazy undulation.

On the ocean side of the atoll giant combers heaved over with a vast sigh as they sounded the long-drawn rumble of their death; but within the charmed circle of the lagoon the surface of the water was scarcely ruffled. Under the soporific power of the sun the distant palms dozed above their shadows in a deep green trance. It was just such a scene as Judd had known from infancy; yet it still had the power to ensorcell him with its magic, to touch him with the emotion of amazement, as if he were seeing earth and sky and sea fresh from the hand of the Creator—the same yesterday, today, and forever.

Conk was trailing his line in blissful disregard of the fact that fish as gorged as these could not be lured with lowly "salt horse." Ken Henderson was busy with his notebooks, lost within his world of petroglyphs and trilithons, of artifacts and pictographs. Terii, whose superb bronze body glistened with spray, seemed one with the elements themselves, a sun-born child of nature. Only Sven Dineson offered a jarring note. Withdrawn into himself, the young Dane's lips moved soundlessly, as if in secret argument. Whatever the nature of his preoccupation, he stiffened suddenly and swung about to face Judd Anders. And it was at once apparent that he had come to some final conclusion. When he spoke a note in his voice caused every head to turn.

"It's this Einar Karlson, Captain," he muttered in a hollow tone.

"What about him?" Judd demanded sharply, and knew, with strange prescience, that he was about to be told something he would not care to hear.

"He calls himself a Dane."

"You believe he's not?"

The other shook his head in gloomy negation.

"But he speaks Danish, doesn't he?" Judd persisted.

"*Ya,* that is the trouble! He speaks it like a gentleman who has been to a fine school. Not like a sailor."

With relief Judd retorted: "Even a gentleman may follow the sea. Nothing else worrying you, Sven?"

"There is more, sir. Karlson has other languages. *Too* well he speaks them! In Auckland he spoke as the English themselves speak—not as I have heard him talk with you aboard ship. And he was always reading French newspapers and German ones too."

"Nothing strange in that," Judd brought out, but his unease was growing. "Tell me, does he know your country well, Sven?"

"Better than myself," the other assented, and his pale eyes seemed to cloud. "He knows the inland country where only the rich may travel. But"—and here Dineson wagged his head—"it is this which puzzles me: Einar Karlson does not know the little things that every Danish child is taught, songs I learned at my mother's knee, games I played. He knows only the fine language.

Not sailor songs or sailor talk. And I believe he has tried to turn the fo'c'sle against me, sir——"

This was a longer speech than Sven Dineson had been heard to utter since the beginning of the voyage. Somehow it convinced Judd of the Dane's integrity. But this very fact convicted the first mate of deception! Details which before seemed inconsequential took swift significance: Einar Karlson's confusion of British and American accents which Judd *had* noticed but had disregarded; the man's arrogance in dealing with underlings—not the dominance of an officer in position to bully, but a sort of involuntary race consciousness of superiority. That Karlson, whatever his origins, had been born above the station he now occupied was unquestionable. And what explanation could be found for the fact that the man was a seaman of wide experience, yet unversed in the "sailor talk" of his native Denmark? Under what flag had he served his apprenticeship?

Quietly Judd brought out: "You believe he's a German. Is that it?"

"Ya, you take the vords off my tongue, sir."

"Why haven't you spoken of this before?"

"Because I had no facts, Captain. Only suspicions. I did not vish to make trouble."

"But Karlson's ship was torpedoed by the Nazis," Judd said slowly. "There were other survivors to bear out the claim."

Dineson shook his head, unconvinced.

Ken interrupted to suggest: "The Colonial Intelligence went over him with an X ray, didn't they? They passed his papers——"

Judd admitted that they had. "Still, the papers could have been forged." Yet it was scarcely credible that, in time of war, the Intelligence could have been so easily hoodwinked. If Karlson's papers were forgeries someone had done a superb job.

"Vun thing more, Captain," Sven Dineson was saying.

"Well?"

"It happened yust a few minutes ago, ven you sent me back to your cabin for the binoculars."

"*What* happened?"

"As you see, my feet are bare. I vent quiet. Einar Karlson vas in your cabin, sir!"

A dozen legitimate errands could explain the mate's presence there. But Judd's mind leaped with instinctive apprehension to the charts, to the logbook locked in the desk. Involuntarily his fingers sought the keys attached to the ring at his belt, as if to draw reassurance from the fact that they were still there.

"Well?" he demanded tersely.

"Karlson vas on hands and knees under the desk vhere you lock the log," the Dane said doggedly. "He seemed to be looking for somet'ing. He did not hear me enter. So surprised vas he that for vonce I think he told the truth."

"What did he say?"

"That he vas looking for a button!"

"A *button?*" the other echoed, incredulous.

"Ya! He showed me vhere a button had pulled off his jacket. They vere odd buttons, Captain."

"What like?"

"Made of real silver, and the figure of a *narvhal* on the top. Many times I have seen such buttons in Denmark, never anyvere else. But they are vorn yust by fine officers."

"Well," snapped Judd, "what does that prove?"

"Nothing to prove, Captain," the Dane muttered gloomily. "I have only suspicions. I felt it my duty to varn you." He hesitated, then brought out: "As for that little Yap——"

"What about the Jap?" Judd demanded.

"He came in the cabin too, to help look for the button, he said. And vhat good's a Yap up to—unless you got two fellows to vatch him?"

"Right on the beam, Swede," Conk agreed with fervor. "And even then they'll steal you blind. You gotta slap their ears down."

"I wish you'd told me what you suspected sooner," Judd said grimly.

"Ya, I have given it much thought. But I do not like to make trouble. I am a man of peace, sir."

Ken interrupted the discussion with a laugh. "Doesn't sound to me like anything to get excited about. A silver button—so what? As for Karlson's accent, any foreigner who learns English can mix up British and American without knowing the difference. You're making mountains out of molehills."

"Perhaps," Judd admitted, willing enough to be convinced, yet plagued still by that sense of unease. Dineson's suspicions proved nothing conclusive but they added a deeper note to the warning tocsin. Slowly the boy brought out: "Ever since we left the ship, Ken, I've had a feeling something was afoot. I don't know what——"

"Stop crystal-gazing, Skipper," the other scoffed. "Be yourself! That black lip is waiting for us and this is our last day."

"Okay . . . I guess you're right."

At that moment the prow of the canoe crunched the shallows, and the whole atoll, beach and palms, seemed to rush forward in the blinding light. Judd lowered the sail on the run. All thought of Einar Karlson and Haru Osaka dissolved in the heat shimmer that wavered upward from the blazing strand.

CHAPTER III Treachery

TERII SPRANG into the shallows to seize the gunwale of
the canoe in his powerful grip while the others went
clambering overside into the sun-warmed water, helping to drag the canoe toward shore, hauling it beyond
tidal reach.

Heat flickered above coral clinkers that felt like live
coals to bare feet, and the glare became a searing ache to
the eyeballs. Near at hand a wild boar crashed through
the undergrowth in snorting alarm, while hermit crabs
snapped into their shells with amazing celerity and
scurried in all directions. At the edge of the jungle a
pile of rotted-out black-lip shell stank to high heaven.
Above it sea birds rose in clouds, raucously protesting

the approach of the intruders. There was something incalculably breathless, remote, and lonely about a scene in which only the human voice seemed alien and intrusive. Like most Pacific atolls, Vana Vana was a series of islets threaded upon a reef to enclose a lagoon. At its highest point the land was scarcely more than six feet above the level of the sea. During aeons of time coral polyps had been building ramparts of limestone to form this lonely atoll, and its immemorial solitude seemed fixed upon it like an unbreakable spell.

A purao raft lay under the shelter of the palms, and Terii was removing the woven mats which protected it from the sun's destructive rays. Conk and Sven Dineson helped to slide the unwieldy raft into the shallows. Immediately it entered its own element, for it floated upon the water as lightly as a resting gull. Three empty wooden packing cases were then dragged out of the bush and carried to the shore's edge.

Sweat rolled down sun-tanned bodies that bent to the labor of packing the heavy, sharp-edged shell. No one spoke. Once Ken shot a surreptitious glance at Judd, who obviously was preoccupied with Sven Dineson's recent disclosure. Easygoing Ken Henderson, whose own thoughts usually went haymaking in the fields of ancient Polynesian lore, couldn't bring himself to believe that anyone as direct as Einar Karlson could be other than he seemed. Judd certainly was borrowing trouble.

The first of the cases was soon filled and nailed,

loaded aboard. In spite of the shell's great weight the raft continued to ride buoyantly upon the ripples, commanding the boys' admiration.

"That purao's like South American balsa," Ken observed. "You can't sink the stuff."

"It *is* as light as balsa," Judd agreed, "but it'll stand a lot more punishment."

"What are we going to do with the raft when we sail —leave it behind?"

"I've been thinking about that. It might come in handy if we lost a smallboat. Guess we'd better take it along."

Days later Judd Anders had good cause to remember that offhand decision, to wonder what would have happened to them all had he never made it.

At that moment, however, he was trying to persuade himself that Ken was right: that his suspicions about Einar Karlson were unfounded; perhaps he *was* making mountains out of molehills. Anyhow, the sooner he got back aboard the *Island Queen* the more relieved he'd be!

Terii straightened up from his labors, glistening with sweat. His broad brown face broke into a childlike grin as he tested with one huge thumb the bright edge of his machete. "That wild pig we heard," he suggested slyly. "*Aiá*, American, but fresh pork would be good to taste!"

Reluctantly Judd frowned down the idea, even though fresh meat would be a welcome change from the monotony of the salt horse, the hardtack, and duff which would comprise the ship's fare on the return voyage to Honolulu.

"But I, Terii à Mautaua, am the greatest hunter in the valley of Upolu!" the native cried reproachfully. "I can track and slay that pig in one hour's time!"

Stubbornly Judd shook his head. "We've got to finish this job and get back to the ship as soon as possible."

Thus they all labored at top speed throughout the remaining hours of the morning—one of the few occasions when Judd had invoked his authority as ship's captain, but he felt that circumstances warranted it. He couldn't throw off the belated conviction that he had been lax where he should have been vigilant; that his instinctive trust in other men's good intentions might have betrayed them all.

Ken, with less physical endurance than his mates, finally voiced feeble protest. "What's the sweatshop idea, Skipper? If we don't get away on tonight's ebb there's always tomorrow."

"I've got more reasons than black lip for wanting to get back to the ship," came the short answer.

"Still crystal-gazing?"

"Could be."

By noon the sun had grilled the beach to an inferno of heat and glare. Then only, with the work almost completed, did the young skipper call a halt. And welcome it was. The protective shade of the coconut fronds that tossed above their heads allured them, while Terii twisted a vine about his ankles and set his broad feet at the base of a palm he intended to climb. Gripping the trunk with both hands, up he went, agile as a monkey. A hundred feet above the beach he twisted at the wire-like stems of green coconuts, until nut after nut dropped with dull thud to the sand. A flash of Judd's machete, and great green goblets were passed around with a drink for all. Cool and effervescent on the hottest days, the coconut liquid was nectar to parched throats. The surrounding bush yielded mangoes, guavas and mummy apples, oranges and bananas. An inexhaustible supply of food and drink seemed to be at hand for the reaching. With countless thousands of nesting sea birds, boars, and wild chickens, a lagoon teeming with fish, it seemed that Nature had smiled indulgently upon Vana Vana.

"Are white men saps!" Conk McCoy was heard to murmur. Reclining against the bole of a palm, allowing cool juices to trickle down his throat, he broke off long enough to sigh: "All a guy has got to do is grab his dinner off a tree. I've a mind to stay here the rest o' my life."

"What would you do without your comics?" Ken grinned.

"You've got something there, Professor. I like to know what Superman's up to."

It was decided that Terii and Sven Dineson should paddle the raft and the three cases back to the ship, with Judd and the others returning by canoe. The wind had shifted and Judd knew that the afternoon would be far gone before they regained the brig. Even with a head start the awkward raft would make slow going. And the boy's impatience sharpened. If they lost the ebb it would be necessary to lay over another night; and now, faced with growing uncertainty, he was anxious to get under weigh.

It was two hours later before those in the canoe, rounding a spur of land, caught sight of the *Island Queen.* Anxiously Judd scanned her through his binoculars. Plenty of activity aboard. An indubitable air of departure. Men aloft were bent over the yards, others running up and down the web of shrouds. Efficient mate that he was, Karlson would have the brig ready to sail as soon as the last of the cases was hoisted aboard.

Judd's professional eye warmed to shining brightwork, trim yards and spars, neat flemish coiling of lines. All was shipshape. And the boy tingled in response to the emotion that his ship always evoked in him: she was sweet as a nut and sound as a bell; as close and vital to him as a loved human being. He could not envision a future for himself in which the *Island Queen* played no part. Every one of her fine points he knew and exulted in, and he refused to recognize a single fault!

The canoe slid alongside. Karlson could be seen waiting by the rope ladder, his face inscrutable as always. From the direction of the galley came Haru Osaka's voice raised in song, like the shrilling of a peanut vendor's whistle.

The first mate touched his cap respectfully as Judd

clambered aloft. "The raft, sir?" And the man's tone was deferential. "Is it to be cut adrift?"

"We're taking it," Judd returned, and shot the other a quick look. "Have it hoisted for'ard."

"Aye, aye, sir." No shadow of emotion showed in the cold eyes.

"We'll weigh anchor as soon as Terii gets here with the shell. He's rounding the point now."

"The tide is about to set, sir. Everything is ready. Ve vill not miss the ebb."

As Karlson issued the order to have the canoe dismasted and hoisted aboard Judd noted the alacrity with which the men leaped to obey. And the boy was forced to concede that there had been no malingering; that, with some special skill, the first mate had whipped these jailbirds into creditable seamen who jumped in answer to command.

In his cabin Judd went immediately to the chart locker and unlocked it. Each chart, rolled and tied, appeared to be exactly as he had left it. This point he checked for certainty, since there was a definite order in which he replaced the charts after consulting them. He could have taken his oath that this sequence had not been disturbed. Vastly relieved, the boy turned toward the desk where the log was locked. But at that moment Terii's voice could be heard hailing the brig, and a glance through the porthole disclosed a glimpse of the raft with its precious cargo. The log would have to wait; Judd hurried aloft to superintend the stowing of the last three cases.

The hatch was uncovered, the stench of black lip radiated from the brig's hold, overpowering in the hot air. Block and tackle had been rigged, and as soon as the raft pulled alongside and made fast, the heavy cases were hoisted aboard. Terii and Sven Dineson clambered up the rope ladder, weary with the struggle of paddling the heavily laden raft against a head wind. Haru Osaka, dish towel in hand, emerged from the galley; his broad face was beaming, doubtless in happy anticipation of wedding bells so soon to ring in Honolulu.

In jig time the heavy cases were swayed into the hold, the hatch again battened down, the entire operation moving with the precision of clockwork. The raft was stowed forward.

Then the first mate turned to Judd Anders, and his rare smile relieved momentarily the habitual coldness of his face. "That does it, sir," he said.

"Good work, mister! Get off the gaskets, then. Heave short! Stand by with the smallboat to tow if necessary."

"Aye, aye, sir."

Orders were bawled thick and fast. Men sprang to obey. Brown arms hauled. Slowly the anchor rose from its bed of sand where it had rested these five months, and the air was rent with a rousing chantey. Terii, master helmsman, was assigned to the wheel; he flipped the spokes, sniffed the wind, and eyed the sky, stalwart as some heroic Viking out of the Age of Bronze.

As the mainsail set and began to fill, the *Island Queen*

swung slowly in a wide curve, gathering momentum as she moved toward the reef passage, impelled by the running flow of the tide and the breeze that came hauling out of the south. With each second the ebb gathered speed and volume. It raced through the narrow opening into a cross-sea of conflict, to meet at last the tides of the outer ocean. A steady hand was called for, a knowing eye, to guide a ship of this beam and draught through such a narrow passage. The smallest miscalculation would have sent the brig to destruction on the sharp-toothed coral. But Terii's keen eye estimated exactly the ebb's speed, gauged the ship's response; and so perfect was his sense of timing that at the moment of the ebb's swiftest volume the brig was lined up dead center for the passage.

The *Island Queen* shot through like a deer with the hounds at her heels, lumbered across the agitated waters of the cross-sea, settled in her new course. And the long-rolling swells of the Pacific rose to greet her like an old friend. She lifted to them with as little effort as a gull in its flight. Sea birds raced at the main-truck, their cries a raucous screeching. Against the sky the Stars and Stripes streamed from the peak of the gaff; and Judd Anders, glancing aloft, felt the thrill which that sight always evoked within him: his country's flag, so jaunty and challenging against the sky.

At the taffrail he and Ken turned their gaze back toward the low-lying ring of coral that had held so much of adventure for them. The atoll dropped from sight rapidly, each second slipping farther and farther beyond the reverse curve of blue Pacific. Soon it would be entirely lost to sight—an imminence that left both boys solemn, for they knew that something exciting had come to an end, an experience they could never quite repeat.

Turning, Ken said: "How did you find everything below, Skipper?" And his tone was half serious, half mocking.

"All right, near as I could tell."

The other chuckled. "How about our Benedict Arnold?"

"Maybe it *was* just crystal-gazing, Professor. I'll see you at chow. Got to write up the log now."

"Okay, Skipper."

In his cabin the desk drawer slid easily as Judd turned the key. A sheaf of papers fluttered to the floor as the boy lifted out the heavy book; but in that second his eye was distracted by a spot of color on the calendar above his desk. In blood-red crayon someone had drawn a circle around December seventh. Had Ken, in his absent-minded fashion, used that device to remind himself of some obligation? Probably. But suddenly Judd stiffened. For he knew that Ken had not come below since returning to the brig! Who, then, had drawn the red circle? And why?

The boy's fingers were unsteady as he opened the heavy book. In so doing a round flat object fell to the floor with a metallic tinkle, gave a bright gleam.

Quickly Judd reached for it. But already he knew what it was: *a silver button*. It had been *inside* the drawer, somehow caught in the log and ship's papers. He knew there would be a narwhal at the top of the button.

He felt the blood drain from his face, heard his heart thump to pump it up again. So Einar Karlson possessed a key to the desk! If the mate was able to consult the log, then surely he had access to the charts as well. The exact bearings of Vana Vana were a secret no longer. Judd found himself thinking clearly in a maelstrom of emotions. If Karlson owned skeleton keys, doubtless he'd availed himself of the firearms locker at the end of the corridor. Another thought rocked the boy on his heels as his eyes sought the secret bulkhead over the desk. It worked with a trick spring, concealing a compartment in which were kept ship's funds and secret papers, some stick dynamite and caps. Only Judd and Ken knew the existence of the secret panel. A glance assured Judd that it had not been tampered with, for once the panel was opened it was impossible for anyone to close it who didn't know the combination.

Swiftly the boy moved toward the door and down the corridor. The great brass deadlock of the firearms locker gleamed dully in the half-light. Had Karlson been in here too? Immediately he understood what had happened: the door's hinges had been removed, then screwed back into position. There was even a flake of paint on the floor which had escaped someone's attention. All this had been done that very morning while

Judd and his companions were loading shell. Karlson and Osaka had scarcely waited for the canoe to clear the ship; Dineson had all but caught them red-handed. But why had Karlson waited until the last case was stowed before showing his hand?

In direct answer to that question a voice grated: "Raise your hands, Kapitan!"

A muzzle of steel bored the base of Judd Anders' spine, and there sounded a deliberate well-oiled click as a cartridge slid from the magazine. Slowly the boy's arms came up. The mate's free hand passed quickly over his hip pockets.

"You may turn around now, Kapitan," the harsh voice said, and the final word underscored deliberate affront.

Judd wheeled to face the blued steel of a big automatic, recognized it for his own. Instantly it was all clear but he managed to bring out: "What's the meaning of this, Karlson?"

"*Ach*, you are a bigger *dummkopf* than I thought!"

"You speak in German now."

"*Ja*, my smart friend. The language of the master race." The Danish accent miraculously had vanished, its place taken by a clipped British inflection, interlarded with German.

The boy knew an intolerable impulse to smash that treacherous face between the eyes.

The other read the impulse, sneered: "I wouldn't try it, Kapitan. It would be a pleasure to kill you, but the time is not yet. . . ."

At that second a shot rang out overhead. The corridor reverberated with the detonation.

Karlson smiled. "One taken care of!"

Blood pounded in Judd's throat. "What have you done?"

"We will see who was the first to go," the mate leered. "Step ahead of me and no tricks, mind!"

The pistol prodded Judd's spine as, blinking, he emerged into the brilliant sunshine of the deck. The scene that met the boy's eyes was like the materialization of a bad dream—so terrible that his mind momentarily refuted the evidence of his sight. Sven Dineson's body was stretched flat on the planking. A trickle of blood oozed from a hole in the center of the young Dane's forehead. Terii, Ken, and Conk were standing elbow to elbow, while around them the jailbirds of the crew formed a murderous circle, each man brandishing a rifle from the firearms locker and willing enough to use it. Karlson had done his work well: these were *his* men. Ken's eyes were bewildered behind the horn-rimmed glasses, his sun helmet askew, lending him a ludicrous appearance. Conk's lips were drawn in a defiant scowl, while Terii seemed caught between the emotions of utter disbelief and childlike rage.

Haru Osaka was standing over Sven Dineson's body. The little Oriental was smiling as he broke open his smoking pistol. Calmly he thrust a hand into his pocket, pushed a fresh cartridge into the empty chamber.

Something exploded within Judd Anders. His vision

swam. In a voice strange to his ears he heard himself shouting: "You've killed him!"

"How fortunate it was not you!" Vastly pleased with himself, the little Japanese gave his hissing chuckle. Before these tall white men, his captives, Haru Osaka paraded like a toy soldier. For a second he paused to eye Ken Henderson, knocked the sun helmet still further askew, and in his black glance there was a triumph of insolence. "The master ethnologist," he taunted shrilly, "who cannot tell a Dane from a German!"

It was incredible that this swaggering bantam was the same Haru Osaka who, for five months past, had been the deferential servant anticipating every order, always smiling, respectful. Some current of intolerable hatred had transformed him into a small yellow demon whose eyes blazed with a fire of fanaticism.

Impatiently Einar Karlson clicked back the hammer of his revolver. "Make an end to this, Osaka! You waste our time." The mate's impatience was edged with contempt—the disdain of the self-styled master race for one of another blood. It was manifest that only the bond of expediency existed between these two.

"*I* am in command here," the Japanese reminded his confederate, in a voice all velvet, but the eyes were black pools of danger. "We will make an end, as you suggest. But I shall have the pleasure of deciding what that end will be."

"You'll shoot the swine, of course," the German snapped, "as you shot the Dane."

Treachery

"The Dane was foolish, *so* foolish," Osaka murmured. "These others will not be so fortunate."

"You mean . . . ?"

"They will not be shot!"

"What do you intend to do?"

Coolly the Japanese chose to ignore that question. He addressed himself to the jailbirds: "The raft—put it in the water, you fools! And you, Karlson, will keep these clever young men covered while I relieve them of possessions they will no longer need."

Nimble yellow fingers rifled the boys' clothing, darting, probing, lifting: jackknives, keys, coins, cigarettes, handkerchiefs—their trifling possessions dropped to the deck. Ken's knapsack was yanked rudely from his shoulders, its contents flung overside into the water; his sun helmet was knocked from his head. Judd alone was wearing shoes and these he was ordered to remove; his key ring was tossed contemptuously to Einar Karlson. Terii's scanty pareu yielded only a box of matches and a pandanus cigarette, rolled into a fold of the cloth. Even these were appropriated. The little Japanese was compelled to stretch on tiptoe to wrench the shark knife from the cord about Terii's throat; and for a second it seemed that the giant Polynesian would strike this pygmy to the deck. A sharp warning from Judd, however, caused Terii to drop his arms, but his big fingers opened and closed spasmodically. On his face was an expression no one of them had ever before seen. The knife hit the deck with a ringing *ping*.

49

Again the infuriating chuckle; Osaka was toying with his victims with feline cruelty. "Shooting would be too quick, too painless, too simple," he murmured. "But before your end comes I assure you honorable gentlemen you will wish a thousand times I had put a bullet in your skulls. No, I have a better plan. . . ." Expectantly he paused, and the black eyes held the unwavering glitter of a snake's in the instant before it strikes.

"Get this over with, Osaka," Judd ground out. "We're at your mercy but we're not crawling."

A spasm of rage contorted the yellow features. With the flat of his hand Haru Osaka struck Judd Anders across the mouth. A vicious blow. He spat at the boy's feet.

Judd's vision blurred. His throat swelled. Desperately he fought to bring himself under control, but the effort proved nearly his undoing. "Try that without a gun in your hand, Osaka!"

A derisive snort was the reply. "Ho! The superior white man! You will learn that a white man can die as easily as one of another color. And this day will live in history to prove it! A pity you will not be alive to know how December seventh is a day of everlasting honor for the Mikado, the exalted Son of Heaven——"

Conk McCoy's patience cracked. "Turn over the record, Half Hitch," he snapped. "Let's hear the other side!"

"Mongrel!" Osaka flung at him. "Son of dogs!"

"Call me Conk. It's easy to remember."

For one second it seemed that Conk McCoy would die where he stood. The Japanese held himself in check but the effort was reflected in the momentary unsteadiness of his voice. Now that voice was saying: "I shall tell you honorable gentlemen what your fate is to be. You will be put aboard the raft. Without food. Without water. Shall I make a picture of what it will be like, the way you will die? Your tongues will grow black and swell until they choke in your mouth. Your eyes will be blinded by the sun. Your teeth will come loose and fall. Your skin—it will crack and fester. Still alive, you will become skeletons. Your minds will be the last to go, so that you may taste the full flavor of a death that creeps by inches. Of course"—the hissing chuckle fell lightly—"there are always the sharks. . . ."

The four boys stood rooted, speechless, scarcely believing that their ears were not tricking them; that the words uttered by this small yellow man, this monster who so coolly dictated their fate, could have significance.

"One more matter . . ." Like a merciless swordsman whose rapier seeks the vulnerability of his victim, Osaka whipped toward Judd Anders. "I have seen the foolish pride you take in this ship, *so* foolish. Perhaps you would like to know what her fate will be?"

"Which means you intend to tell me," the other returned levelly.

Osaka's smile reflected the supreme pleasure he enjoyed in finding the boy's most vulnerable spot. Triumphantly he drove the fine blade home. "The *Island Queen* will be sailed to a secret base where she will be turned into a floating powder magazine. As a decoy she will fly the American flag. And always she will appear to be in distress, so that ships coming to her assistance will scarcely have time for regret before they are sent to the bottom. I believe it is what you call a Q-boat. I tell you this because you will never be able to pass on the information and it would be a pity for you not to know."

"You understand, Kapitan," Einar Karlson added, "how much your stupidity will cost your countrymen. This plan was set in operation by our agents in San Francisco as soon as we learned that the Colonial Government had underwritten your expedition. We have permitted you to finish loading the shell because it has fine market value. Our exalted leaders can make use of that good money!"

Judd flared: "But my country is not at war with yours."

"*Donnerwetter!* Your country has sided with my enemies since the beginning. America shall pay high for her stupidity—and for yours."

"You'll never get away with this, Karlson——"

"You won't be alive to know, Kapitan," the other retorted.

Osaka broke in: "Over the side with you honorable gentlemen, or it might be that I change my mind!"

With rifle butts the jailbirds prodded the four boys

toward the scuppers. Terii, in a glower of anger, swung over the rail and dropped to the raft. Sullenly Conk followed; then Ken, still more bewildered than dismayed by the suddenness of events. Something seemed to go dead in Judd Anders, thus to be abandoning the *Island Queen* ignominiously, at the point of a gun. He experienced a crazy impulse to fight it out, to go down with a bullet in his heart, aboard his ship. Wildly he thought of the dynamite behind the secret bulkhead, and knew he'd a thousand times rather see the brig blown to glory than be debased as Osaka intended.

Angrily Einar Karlson shouted: "Step quick, Kapitan!" And his trigger finger trembled.

The wild impulse passed from Judd, leaving him quiet and icy cold. As he swung over the rail and dropped the raft scarcely shifted with his weight. Instantly a boathook shoved the purao clear of the brig. Wind and tide spun it at their whim, as if it were the merest cockleshell upon the waters.

At the brig's rail Einar Karlson and Haru Osaka fingered their pistols, leered broadly as their jailbird confederates pursued the raft with a chorus of taunting catcalls. Rapidly the distance widened, but the little Japanese bridged it to cry: "I wish you a pleasant passage—to hell!"

"We'll be seein' you!" the irrepressible Conk hurled back.

Instantly a spatter of bullets whipped the water beside the raft. "Mongrels! Sons whose ancestors were dogs!" shrilled Osaka.

"Same to you and in bunches!" Conk yelled.

Another bullet sent a splinter of wood flying. Judd gripped Conk's arm. "Skip it!" he warned. "A live dog's better than a dead lion."

"Lion? I feel like a duck in a shooting gallery."

The *Island Queen's* topsails filled as she stood toward the northwest, breasting the swells with that same winged buoyancy the boys knew and loved so well. They strained after their vanishing ship with their heart in their eyes, while a chaos of emotions struck them silent. Suddenly, as they watched, the American flag was lowered. In its place another flag was hoisted to the peak of the gaff: the emblem of the Rising Sun, flaunting insolently on the breeze. It dipped twice—a mocking salutation. Something stung on Judd Anders' eyelids; resolutely he averted his gaze.

Quietly he said: "Square away, mates."

Within an hour the brig was hull-down on the horizon and pulling away fast. One by one her square-rigged topsails disappeared beyond the flawless rim of the Pacific. And seeking so desperately a final glimpse of their ship, the boys fought down the words that rose involuntarily in their throats.

Only Judd spoke. "There she goes, mates. The last we'll ever see of her!"

It was the bitterest moment of his life.

CHAPTER IV Challenge of the Sea

THE STARS had lost their fire and were dead. Out of the low-hanging mists the sea emerged, blue and violent. Though the sun had not yet risen, the eastern sky was striped with bands of angry yellow, warning of a new day. In that hostile expanse of ocean and sky the little raft and its occupants appeared incalculably forsaken.

Sitting watch, Conk McCoy shivered in the morning mists. His wet shirt and shorts were plastered to his chilled body. His teeth chattered. "Doggone," he muttered hungrily, easing cramped muscles, "does that sky look like a scrambled egg! And could I do with one!"

Ken lifted on one elbow to grumble: "Better be glad you're alive. By rights you ought to be dead."

"Thanks, pal, I like it better this way." Conk raised his voice to shout: "First call for breakfast! Come a-runnin'!"

"Oh, pipe down!"

Their voices roused Judd. In the second required to get his bearings, the boy realized that he had dozed fitfully after the long ordeal of his watch; and while he had slept the events of the preceding day had re-created themselves in his dreams, phantoms so vivid that he could still hear Haru Osaka's infuriating chuckle, almost see the icy glint of Einar Karlson's stare.

From long habit the boy swept the empty horizon with his glance. No distant sail, no telltale smudge of a steamer's smoke. Even the reflection thrown up on the lower sky by Vana Vana's lagoon—the "sky fire" of the Polynesians—had vanished. The atoll might never have existed. This area of the Pacific was far removed from the narrow shipping lanes. To expect the miracle of being picked up by a passing ship was to clutch at a straw. Knowing that his companions fully understood this, Judd refrained from attempting to boost their morale with false hope. They had voted confidence in his judgment; he must be on guard to do or say nothing which might undermine that faith.

The boy knew that the waters in these latitudes had never been extensively charted. Many shoals not recorded were unknown by the cartographer and undiscovered by the mariner except those luckless enough to run afoul them. In this treacherous region a man must, perforce, sail his ship "by guess and by God." Would Einar Karlson be lucky enough to navigate the *Island Queen* safely to the secret base Osaka had bragged about? Where could that base be? A thousand possibilities existed in this vast Pacific area. For the past twenty-five years Japan had been developing the islands under her mandate, building fortifications whose true character no white man had discovered and lived to reveal to the outside world.

At thought of his ship, his beautiful swift ship, Judd winced inwardly. He never expected to lay an eye on her again; the ignominious use to which she was being subjected, luring to destruction vessels of his own country, was something he could not bear to think about. Perhaps—he sought to console himself—some armed merchantman warier than others would see through Osaka's ruse and send the *Island Queen* to the bottom. Such a possibility he almost welcomed.

Conk McCoy was asking, "Who's got a cigarette?" and so bemused was Judd that involuntarily he found himself reaching for his hip pocket. "Just smoked the last one, Conk," he said with sheepish pretense.

"I'll do the same for you sometime," the other promised. "Say, how about a slice o' bacon with your eggs, Skipper?"

"How about soaking your head?"

"There ain't water enough."

Terii made a sweeping gesture toward the east, as one who introduces a new character in a drama. "*Te mahana!*" he stated. "The sun comes to us, Americans. It is good."

"And about time," muttered Conk. "My bones are frozen."

"They'll thaw before noon," Judd reminded him dryly.

Somehow the sun filled them all with hope. After the bleak hours of the night, the anxiety which had been a portion of each one's thoughts in the weary interval of his watch, here was the sun rising to sweep the mists from the sea. It came as a friend to set their spirits lifting. It made them believe that God had not forsaken them; that being together on a raft, drifting with wind and current, might somehow prove to be a thrilling adventure. Only Judd understood how relentlessly that sun could become an enemy.

On a raft measuring eight feet by ten there was little chance of trimming the weight of three boys whose height was above average, plus a fourth of herculean proportions. Terii's superior weight necessitated relegating him to the "stern," which lent a corresponding lift to the raft's "bows." But as the interminable hours passed they all began to be obsessed by the irresistible impulse to move, even if only for a few inches. Muscles accustomed to active use ached with the strain of inaction.

With each minute the color of the sea intensified—water whose unbelievable blue, so strongly saline, had its source in the high evaporation of the tropics, since water of lesser salt content is green. In this clear element fish could be seen playing about the raft, attracted by the lure of its shining whiteness. The ocean was teeming and alive with infinite variety in color and form, many of the species foreign to Judd's knowledge and even to Terii's. Here was a realm to drive the icthyologist to distraction, to send him scurrying down paths of blind research for specimens never before seen or recorded. Dolphins, those speediest swimmers of the southern ocean, went racing after their prey, the flying fishes; and it was sheer delight to follow their progress, to watch those elongated bodies shooting forth like torpedoes from some mighty battery. One of them, possessed by a spirit of play, vaulted high into the air, whirled like a harlequin, smacked the water with a broadside that could be heard half a mile away. Nearer at hand a fleet of gargantuan sting rays, looking like aquatic bats, flapped their wings in flight, lashing the water to fury. At the other end of the scale the iridescent nautilus drifted past in flotillas of sun-shot bubbles, trailing those dangerously deceptive streamers which floated like gossamer.

And always the sharks—blue sharks of deep water, ranging in size from twelve to twenty feet. Their inseparable escort of pilot fish, as round as cigars and banded with black, swam freely beside the jaws of their masters. So far the sharks seemed content to maintain a wary distance from the raft, biding their time—a sinister escort and one it wouldn't do to think too much about.

Terii eyed them hungrily, for the blue shark made good eating. Aiá! For his shark knife! With that in hand, Terii could have accounted for one less *ma'o* in the sea and food aplenty for his companions.

Conk McCoy decided to rig a fishline, declaring that it was "dumb" to watch your breakfast swimming around and do nothing about it.

"But what'll you use for a hook?" Ken wanted to know.

"Don't need a hook, Professor. These tropical boys will snap at any color that's bright. Then you just haul 'em in before they change their little minds. The skipper don't know it yet but he's givin' me the pocket of his dungaree jacket for bait. Such a nice blue! And you, Terii—how's for chewin' me off another piece o' that sennit? Which reminds me, your belt buckle, Professor, would make a swell sinker!" Conk had everything lined up. The way things looked now, he hadn't too long to live and he wasn't going to waste time loafing.

Terii produced a length of sennit which, when shredded into separate strands, became a long stout cord. Baited with blue denim and weighted with a nickel buckle, the coconut sennit fishline presented a grotesque appearance which, in Conk's sight, was a handsome achievement.

"I've heard of catching bullfrogs with red flannel," chuckled Ken, "but these fish are going to die laughing!"

"I won't forget you was a doubtin' Thomas, Professor, when the fish course is served," Conk said with dignity.

The line dropped overside. And dubious though the others were of its success, they watched the buckle gleam and dim as it descended in the sea, felt their mouths water at the prospect of breakfast. For already hunger was gnawing at their healthy young vitals. A meal which of necessity would have to be eaten raw would be no hardship to Terii; nor to Judd Anders, accustomed as the boy was to the numerous raw seafoods of the Tahitians. But Ken Henderson, Chicago-born and -bred, could not suppress a civilized qualm at thought of a wet and slippery meal fresh-caught from the sea, with nothing more potent than will power to coax it down. He'd have to be hungrier than this to swallow fish raw!

There came a tremendous pull on the line. Conk let out a yell and hauled in hand over hand. The line went suddenly slack. It had been sliced in half. Bait and buckle had vanished.

"Doggone, somebody got a breakfast!" Conk exploded.

"Belt buckles on the. half shell," Ken added almost gratefully.

Though he was to fish for many patient hours after that first attempt, Conk McCoy never had another bite.

With torturing deliberation the sun moved up a sky which took on a harder sheen from hour to hour. It arched above their heads, vibrating and pale, seeming never to have known a cloud. Long before noon the heavens had become a blazing dome of metal which, like some vast convex mirror, distorted and flung back the dazzling glitter of the water. Judd pulled off his shirt and tore it into four strips, out of which a weird but partially effective head covering was fashioned for each one. By dousing these rags constantly in the water they achieved a small measure of protection from the sun's violence, but their eyes knew no relief from the million-faceted glare of the sea. At intervals they sluiced water over one another, soaked their garments, only to feel them dry and become salt-caked within seconds.

To Judd the most urgent problem was the necessity of establishing some control over the raft's sailing direction. So far the wind had held true, but it was not the boy's intention to be left at the whim of quixotic elements.

"We'll have another try at that plank, mates," he ordered. "If we're going to reach the Solomons it'll be with a rudder."

Conk groaned, but spat on his hands and said, "Let's go."

Once again the four of them set about the task whose accomplishment was so vitally important. For a full hour they labored, dizzy with heat and fruitless effort; but there was no leverage to help loosen those deep-driven spikes, no object with which to lift and pry— only fingers fumbling for a hold, made slippery by sweat and brine. It proved a hopeless task that once again forced Judd to admit a checkmate and call a halt.

Grimly he eyed the plank. "But we'll get you yet," he swore. "And two more like you for oars."

"You tell 'em, Skipper," groaned Conk. "Words fail me."

This matter of a rudder concerned Terii less than it did Judd Anders. Behind the native's dark eyes lay a knowledge long since forgotten by civilized man: the instinctive wisdom of those whose heritage is bounded by sea and sky. Some sensitivity of the inner ear informs them of atmospheric change; some instinct akin to that of the homing pigeon or the wandering albatross directs them to their goal. As all Samoans, Terii was proud of springing from the race which first peopled the southeastern Pacific. Toward the dark-skinned Fijian, the black Papuan, the fuzzy-haired "eaters of men," the Polynesian had the scorn of inborn superiority.

"It is not only the wind which favors us," Terii was pointing out. "The Ara Moana, River of the Sea, helps us also." And he indicated the masses of weed which, heavy with the eggs of fishes, were drifting rapidly past the raft, always to the southwest.

"Hidden rivers are in the ocean," the native stated in a tone beyond contradiction. "Swift are their currents. Sometimes they run side by side but in opposite directions. East and west, north and south they flow, like highways of the land. It is said that they lead to the end of the world."

Conk's expression indicated that he felt his leg being pulled. "Okay, Terii," he scoffed. "Now *I'll* tell one.

Once upon a time there was a fish called a swamp-swingle. Well, sir, this fish——"

But Judd interrupted this flight of fancy to substantiate Terii's claim for the great ocean currents which had led the first Polynesian navigators from the Asiatic mainland to island after island in the Pacific. "How those boys could sail!" he exulted. "They left the coast of India, followed the path of migratory birds, trusted to the stars and their own good luck—long before the magnetic compass had been introduced from China by Arab traders."

"The first migration was about the second century A.D.," Ken interpolated in his most professional manner.

Between them Conk was reduced to inarticulation; still slightly incredulous, he was content to listen as Judd expanded the subject.

"At home there was an old Tahitian who had names for over a hundred stars. He knew their positions, the time they rose at different seasons of the year. He knew the islands they passed over. And he used to tell me about the hidden rivers of the sea. The Great Black Current, for example, that he called Kuoro Sivo. It sweeps up from the south, curves westward past New Guinea and Celebes, and finally circles back toward Hawaii. Even without sail or paddle, a raft like this could ride such a current at a good pace."

"Ai," assented Terii. "He speaks truth. From the beginning my people followed the roads of the sea, the

Ara Moana, gift of Taaroa. *Aué*, great is the wisdom of Taaroa!"

There was no denying the native's observation that their own small craft was in the grip of a southwesterly current, but where that current might bend or curve was beyond his or Judd's knowing. Personally Judd Anders would have preferred rudder or sail to the more dubious gift of the mythical Taaroa.

An idea suddenly was born in the boy: why not spend a part of each day drawing upon Terii's fund of instinctive wisdom, and at the same time impart to the others his own knowledge of winds and currents, of cloud formations? He could teach them the principle of dead reckoning; how to observe the flight of land-based birds. Why not? Who could foretell what accident might occur at any minute? A single wave sweeping the raft could carry Judd Anders or Terii to Davy Jones's locker, and then how would Conk and Ken Henderson fare? Moreover, such discussions would occupy their minds, speed the hours, helping to crowd back the despair which could rise to sap their will more surely than hunger or thirst.

The others fell in readily with the scheme, acknowledging the wisdom of it.

"Boy, this takes me back," crowed Conk. "The class will come to order. Have we all washed behind the ears this morning? Our first subject, children——"

"Will be the red-tailed tropic bird." Judd grinned. "There are three of them right over your head now,

Conk, and they know more about navigation than you or I are likely to. You see," he went on, "they're 'fine-weather' birds who never travel in a storm. They take off from their bases early in the morning and always return at sunset. If you follow their flight at dusk they'll lead you straight to land."

With satisfaction Judd noted that he'd caught Conk's interest right at the start, and he warmed to his subject, pointing out the remarkable habit of the skimmer birds which were all around the raft, flying close enough to the water to plow a furrow with their bright-colored beaks.

"Why do they keep their mouths closed?" Conk objected. "How can they feed?"

"Their red bills lure small fish to the surface," Judd pointed out. "Notice how the bird doubles back on its tracks and picks up the fish."

"Foxy, huh?"

But of all the birds that planed above their heads, usually approaching upwind and swooping low to peer with curious eyes at the raft and its occupants, the flight of the frigate bird was the most fascinating to follow. This freebooter of the skies was a jaunty fork-tailed marauder who traveled with a rakish speed.

"He's another land-based bird," Judd went on. "Never catches his own fish. Just waits till he sees a booby who has made a good haul, then, being faster on the wing, he makes a dive at the booby and forces him to drop his catch. The frigate snatches the food before it can fall into the sea."

"It's a racket," Conk admired. "There ought to be a law."

"The odd part of it is that ashore these birds pay no attention to each other: they're on equal terms. So stow this fact away, mates—the frigate cannot spend the night at sea. Hence the direction of his flight at sunset will be toward land. The early Polynesians used to take them along as a sort of compass. When you see half a dozen of them together you'll know land is certainly within a hundred miles."

Gulls, quarreling noisily, also testified to the fact that Vana Vana was still within flying range of a shore-based bird; for as Judd pointed out, with the exception of the ocean-going kittiwake, the gull is an inshore bird.

"While you are at sea level, remember that these birds can reach great altitude. With their keen vision they can spot land from a great distance."

"Still," Ken objected, "that doesn't explain away the instinct for unerring direction. Even primitive people have it. I'll bet you could blindfold Terii, spin him in circles, yet he'd still box the compass without a hitch."

Judd agreed. He told the others about the young Tahitian taken aboard by the ubiquitous Captain Cook, who, months later in the East Indies, could point unerringly in the exact direction of his homeland. "He couldn't have done this," the boy explained, "without knowing where the sun was overhead each day, and its position in relation to his home at any season of the year."

"What about the albatross?" Conk wondered. "Aside from bringin' bad luck, what's he good for?"

"No help at all! He sleeps on the ocean and drinks salt water, so he never seeks land except during the breeding season. Even if you're hungry enough to break the superstition and eat him, his flesh is apt to be phosphorescent at night and will scare the liver out of you!"

There was no denying that this classroom discussion had bucked them all up, and Judd vowed that until some miracle brought them food from sea or sky, and rain came to their salvation, he'd keep their minds as active as possible with more of the same diversion.

"Class dismissed for the morning," he grinned. "Don't bother me for a while. I've got to dope out a way to estimate our speed."

The sun reached its zenith. It blasted the raft with stupefying effect, boring down with white-hot wires that penetrated clothing, grilled every patch of exposed human flesh. Hardened though the boys were by exposure, they had never before been forced to accept the sun upon such inescapable terms. The darker pigmentation of Terii's skin afforded the native a measure of immunity lacking to Judd and Ken, while Conk McCoy owned the redhead's unhappy susceptibility to the sun's actinic power. By noon his bare shoulders and his unprotected knees had been broiled to a painful lobster-red; his face was puffy and swollen.

When presently he could endure it no longer, Conk peeled off undershirt and shorts and slid into the sea, gripping the side of the raft as he dunked his fevered body up and down. Ken, eager to follow suit, was halted by Terii's peremptory warning: "Ma'o! Ma'o!"

The dreaded shark cry. It brought Conk back on the raft at a single bound, while Ken's interest instantly evaporated. For a dark shape came racing through the water like a torpedo, and with as deadly an intent. Thwarted, the shark executed a rapid turn, rolled to expose the dull gleam of its belly and a gape of jaw filled with wicked teeth. Measured with the raft as a yardstick, it was not more than five or six feet long, and of the spotted variety known as leopard.

"Boy!" gasped Conk. "Was I playin' squat tag with death! No more of the same if I broil like a wiener."

"That kind are not man-eaters," Judd sought to reassure him.

"Says who?"

"A chap named William Beebe, for one."

"Never heard of him."

"He's an authority on such matters."

"H'mph! Too bad he ain't here to give us a demonstration. Say, who's he look like anyway?"

"Who's *who* look like?"

"That shark."

"Can't say as the face is familiar."

"I've got it!" Conk's eyes sparkled. "With a mustache he'd be the spittin' image of Adolf Hitler!"

And it was a fact that the cold fishy eye, the long-pointed nose, came close enough to caricature to tickle the ribs of them all.

"Little Adolf," chuckled Conk, "runnin' true to form."

Oddly enough, from that moment the shark became the raft's inseparable escort, being distinguishable from others of its kind by a triangular piece of flesh that had been torn from the high fluke of its tail in some bloody encounter. They came to watch for Little Adolf at sunrise, to recognize him as a part of the inescapable pattern, like sun and thirst, like dawn and dark. They came to believe that he alone jolted the raft so rudely during the eerie watches of the night—though this belief was a fancy born of long hours of solitary thought. In any case Little Adolf soon became the very personification of their misfortune; and they hated with fierce hatred that tattered fluke, even as they came to watch for it.

Judd had finally hit upon a crude but effective device for approximating the raft's speed: he tore a few threads of sennit from the remnants of Conk's fishline, threw them ahead into the water as far as possible; then as they swept past the raft (ten feet being the known factor) he counted seconds by the one-and, two-and, three-and, four-and method. However fallible, he was able to work out an approximation of the drift and was amazed to discover how steady was the pull of the mysterious ocean current which held the raft in its grip, bearing it onward to a destiny as yet unknown. But for this current, they might have made their way back to Vana Vana.

Thus the second day edged to a close, drawing the boys together in a single purpose of survival; binding them into a closeness of comradeship which would have been unlikely on land, where differing interests and standards inevitably would have taken them on separate ways.

In silence they watched the blood-red sun burn its way into the sea. A mass of purple clouds assumed the shapes of towers and minarets, behind which bursts of ragged flame shot high into the sky, like the conflagration of some dying city. And the imminence of another night touched each boy's heart with chill fingers. They felt suddenly and forever imprisoned within the rigid walls of the sky, without a rift in the flawless precision of the horizon through which they could hope to escape. Dawn and sundown—the only variety in a round where time flickered like a moving picture without a story. At this hour dry throats and empty bellies made themselves more sharply felt; the stiffness of inaction fixed itself in muscle and bone and spirit.

High overhead a flock of frigate birds went winging eastward, straight as a dark-ruled line against a glow of flame and glory.

"Where do you figure they're headed, Skipper?" Conk wondered.

"Vana Vana."

71

"Lucky ducks!" Conk followed the birds' flight, yearning after them, and the light was slow to fade from his eyes. He sighed, then rallied. His lips gave a wry twist. "This goin' without chow gets you right between the equator and the international date line," he chuckled.

Judd produced the stub of pencil; for this was the hour when they had been set adrift, and he reckoned each new day as beginning and ending at this time. On the chart the boy marked what he estimated to be the component direction and distance of the day's progress. In utter silence, clamoring with thoughts, his companions watched a second firm line take its place beside the first.

Another day had passed. The same question lay unspoken on the lips of each one: how many more such days would come and go?

"My watch, mates," Judd said shortly. "Get some sleep if you can."

CHAPTER V Enemy Sun

DAWN HAD BECOME part of a pattern as everlasting as
the sea itself. The sun came up to warm chilled bodies,
renewing hope, persuading the boys to believe for a few
brief moments that it wished them well. But not for
long could they so delude themselves. By now they had
learned that this treacherous foe came in the guise of a
friend bearing gifts in both hands—gifts of destruction.

Despite this certainty they preferred daylight to dark;
for night was filled with terrors whose very invisibility
added to the sum of fear: sharks bumping against the
raft's bottom; rainless squalls; waves unseen until they
struck without warning, to keep them clutching at life
lines with hands numbed with the strain.

While not yet in actual suffering from the effects of thirst or hunger, their mouths and throats were achingly dry and it was becoming painful to swallow. Lack of moisture cracked their lips where fever blisters formed, adding to their misery.

"If I had a quart o' water right now," said Conk, "it'd take a pint to fill up the cracks before the rest started down my gullet."

It became a mounting aggravation to be forced to watch the birds of the air and the fish of the sea gorging themselves, while they alone lacked means to wrest food from either element. Albatross and frigate, dolphin, shark, and barracuda—each pursued the prey whose capture added one more link to the ageless chain of survival. Only *they*, superior men, must lie helpless and watch, and envy.

That fifth morning as Judd marked on the chart his estimate of the night's drift the eyes of the others eagerly sought the circle to the southwest which, to them, meant more than the Solomon Islands—meant fresh water and food, untroubled sleep, shelter from this blasting inferno of heat and thirst. Safety, solid earth beneath one's feet —did such things really exist? Or were they only empty symbols dreamed up and remembered out of their own great need? Daily they watched their crude chart as men on shore follow the momentous whirl of some wheel of fortune; and they began to place fantastic bets rocketing into thousands as to the number of days and hours, even minutes, to be consumed before reaching their goal.

Conk McCoy's dauntless Irish spirit was never down for long. His greater susceptibility to the sun's rays rendered his discomfort more acute than the others'; but at the lowest ebb of his spirits he could be relied upon to rally, while his companions, however depressed, would play up and soon be laughing. As Ken remarked in a moment of irritation, Conk would doubtless wise-crack on his deathbed. To which the other retorted that, boy, if he could have one night's sleep in an honest-to-gosh bed he'd be willing to die in the morning and keep his mouth shut.

At this moment Conk was thumping the surface of the raft after the manner of an auctioneer on the block. "What am I bid for this swell concrete feather bed?" he demanded. "Don't let it go for a song, ladies and gentlemen. A genuwine antique, reinforced cement with a sandpaper finish. Twenty-five cents, do I hear? Who'll make it thirty? Don't sit on your hands! Going, going . . ."

He had set the ball rolling. Conversation quickly shifted to the subject closest to their hearts: food. Ken recalled the Chicago drugstore around the corner from the museum, where frosted milk shakes were served in glasses a foot tall, and three-decker grilled cheese sand-wiches melted like butter on your tongue.

"I hope the juke box didn't play 'Rocked in the Cradle of the Deep,' " muttered Conk. "That would've spoiled my appetite. Doggone, I know a hash house in Frisco that gives you the works for two bits, and second helpin's don't cost a nickel more. Boy, the steaks I've worked on there! Thick as your arm, with red juice runnin' out of 'em, and all the spuds you can hold: French fried, mashed, or plain boiled." He groaned in an ecstasy of recollection, hugged his empty belly.

Terii and Judd between them painted a Polynesian *luau*—a feast to rock them back upon their heels. In tantalizing detail they lingered over the great pig stuffed with succulent herbs and roasted on red-hot stones; the rivulets of juices running down its sides; the draughts of sparkling effervescent coconut water; the platters of luscious mountain bananas; the altogether delectable *lomi-lomi i'a*.

"What's *that?*" Conk demanded suspiciously.

"Raw salmon pickled in lime juice," he was informed.

"Don't say fish to me, buddy. I never want to see one of the things again."

"I wouldn't pass up a good shark steak right now."

"*Raw?*" Ken demanded feebly.

"I'll say! Even a slice of Little Adolf wouldn't go begging."

Thus they carried on. Food—a perpetual magnet to draw their thoughts irresistibly. They could not keep away from the subject. Again and again they returned to it, as the tongue seeks an aching tooth.

It was during these hours of early morning, before the power of the sun blasted them into silence, that they enjoyed their closest companionship, recalled incidents out of childhood, spoke of hopes longed for and sometimes fulfilled.

Once Conk told them about his early years at the orphanage. "The matron, she was a good egg," he mused, "but she always swore I'd end on the gallows." His gaze wandered out over wastes of empty sea, and he chortled: "Boy, is the joke gonna be on her!"

He told how, at fourteen, a job delivering groceries opened up new worlds; for he entered the homes of the rich. Sometimes a cook or a butler allowed him to peek into the living room. "Jeepers, there was one place had carpets so deep I sank into 'em up to the ankles. Like walkin' on flypaper. There was paintin's all over the walls too—none of your saints and such—but pictures of foreign countries and bridges and ships. Wonderful!"

The docks of New York's waterfront had been Conk's playground. He'd learned to swim in the treacherous eddies of East River; acquired the devious skills of the wharf rat, pilfered food from cargoes on the docks, under the very eyes of a flat-footed watchman.

"I was sixteen when I was shanghaied," he wound up. "A hundred miles at sea when I come to—bound for Rio. I'd been conked on the dome and I had a lump like a baseball. From then on they called me Conk. I was christened Vincent, but I ask you, can you figure a guy like me answerin' to a fancy moniker like *Vincent?*"

Sometimes Judd told them about the valley of Punaruu where he'd grown up, of the young Tahitians who'd been like blood brothers and sisters: Night Moth and Man Who Laughs, Enemy Warrior, Ghost Girl, and Beaten to Death. He spoke of Tetua Nui, his foster mother, who, when his own mother died shortly after his birth, had nursed him at her brown breast, bringing him through childhood with her own children. He spoke of the plantation which had belonged to his father and where someday he hoped to return. And he promised them all a royal welcome, a feast beyond their wildest imagining.

There were times when Terii was moved to speak of his prowess as a hunter of wild pig; of that turning point in adolescence when, by standing stock-still on a high mountain precipice, he had met the charge of a murderous boar, allowing the animal to impale itself on the point of the spear. After that feat the village warriors accepted the stripling as one worthy of associating with themselves; and Terii was allowed to wear upon his chest the boar's tusks, proud symbol of manhood attained.

These recollections caused Ken Henderson to shake his head regretfully. "Nothing ever happened to me," he mourned. "My folks died when I was small. I was brought up as Grandma's boy in a big brick house that looked like a millionaire's mausoleum. Full of books and more books. Stuffed owls. Furniture you slid off because it was covered with horsehair. Old servants who talked in whispers. And then a job in a museum full of skulls. Dead things, all of 'em. No adventures. Nothing."

"How. about the time you killed the shark at Vana Vana?" Judd demanded.

"Shucks, that was nothing."

"Just happened to save my life."

"That's what I meant." Ken grinned.

"Here comes Little Adolf," Conk commented. "You're late this morning, *Hofbrau!* No *Wienerschnitzel* today, you bad boy, you."

Their inseparable escort maintained patient parallel with the raft's passage, occasionally varying his tactics by sweeping close enough to look the boys over with his slit-pupiled eye. There was a sort of cocky insolence in Little Adolf's actions, and his jaws seemed perpetually agape in a taunting grin. Conk diverted himself thinking up ways of getting even with this particular shark, but so far no practical method had suggested itself.

The board which might have served as a rudder still resisted all effort to dislodge it. To see it lying there so solidly driven, defying their utmost effort, was infuriating to the boys when it could mean so much. Each morning there was the labor of trying to pry it loose, but the performance was becoming routine and halfhearted with no promise of success.

One by one, as Vana Vana dropped farther away, the birds vanished from the sky. Even the wandering albatross sought the upper ethers and all but disappeared. Sharks relaxed their vigil, and in the dark waters beside the raft the boys watched the sinister shapes torpedo down into the depths. All nature seemed to be holding its breath with appalling stillness. The abysses of sea and sky met in an unattainable horizon, and the little raft became as detached from the earth and as lonely as a planet.

That fifth morning Terii was the first to sense atmospheric change. Some forewarning of impending storm sped down the ancient wires of heredity, for the native sniffed at the wind, eyed the sky, while anxiety furrowed his brow. But as far as the others could discern, there was no visible change in the vast quicksilver of the sea, in the radiating heat that caused them to withdraw into themselves, stifling the effort of conversation, stupefying thought.

It was mid-afternoon before the signs which the barometer of Terii's instinct had sensed became apparent to them all: first a thickening of the air, a sort of mist through which the sun burned like a fading coal but with undiminished violence; a humidity that sent sweat coursing down their bodies, draining their systems of precious reserves of moisture.

In the far distance indigo clouds massed in formation, like battle cruisers preparing to engage. From minute to minute they brought up fresh reserves—a mighty armada moving hull-down into action. They filled the entire northeastern sky, and as the first vanguard began to edge forward, sounding the thunder of big guns, the open ranks closed behind them. In the forefront of that relentless approach the wind came racing in gusts and spurts, like advance patrols searching the weakness of the enemy. One slaty cloud thrust a tentacle downward, while the sea rose to meet it in a spinning waterspout that whirled toward the raft with subdued roar. Nothing could be done about it. Grimly the boys avoided one another's eyes, fixing their attention upon that whirling vortex of water. They could only watch in awed fascination, and pray. Hundreds of feet high, thicker than the mightiest tree, the spout was inky-dark with a kind of greenish pallor at its heart. It moved with incredible speed across the waves, churning up the sea with a noise like that of an express train. Even when it collapsed, half a mile distant, the mist of it reached them on the wind, chill with cold. Their breath escaped through clicking teeth.

Doggedly Judd tested the life lines, trimmed the weight of their bodies on the raft—the only preparations he could make. He understood the quixotic nature of these tropical squalls, knew that they could build out of dead calm to terrifying violence, only to disappear as quickly. But in that moment of violence they were fearsome to experience. How would the raft behave under storm conditions? Her very buoyancy would count against her. Already the swells were lifting her high, cresting and foaming on both sides, before dropping her into the awful calm of the trough.

Eying the oncoming wind, each one braced himself to meet whatever the minutes must bring; they saw it coming from afar, leaping from crest to crest of the waves. Then they heard the first murmur of its approach, like the deep humming of the world's speed. With outstretched arms the boys gripped the life lines, hooked their feet into the lines on the opposite side. No one said much. They sought to conceal the fact that they were definitely scared, pretending that their only concern with those angry clouds was annoyance at wind without rain. The raft began to dip and buck into a northwest swell.

"Boy," muttered Conk grimly, clutching the life lines till his knuckles showed white, "what I think of this cement mixer!"

They all gave up pretense then, took refuge in utter silence. For a moment a livid sun, compressed between steely clouds, shot forth rays of final defiance. Then the walls of steel converged; and this unnatural murky twilight, through which each boy could see his own bloodless face reflected· in the eyes of his companions, was only an added tax on endurance. Now the cloud armada was moving at top speed. Flashes of blue-white fire lashed at the sea, followed by deafening detonations of thunder. Lightning shot its tracer bullets all about them —exploded, crackling in the sea.

The first hard gust of wind struck like the blow of a fist. Under its brutal impact the raft recoiled, took it pluckily, coming back for more. Judd brought into use the makeshift sea anchor rigged out of his dungaree jacket. He'd risked weakening the raft by using another length of sennit, but he felt that necessity counterbalanced the risk. The jacket, soaked through and tied to one end of the raft, proved momentarily sufficient to swing the light purao head on into the wind. This, the boy prayed, would keep it from broaching to by presenting to the force of the wind the shorter dimension of the raft.

But the weight of the jacket proved inadequate to offset the power of waves so steadily mounting. The raft began to pitch with wild motion. A green sea caught it forward, swung it clear of the water before allowing it to drop back with a resounding smash. White-faced, the boys gripped the life lines. No one spoke. An avalanche streaked with foam sheeted across the raft—green water, icy cold. Another sea struck unfairly from the opposite quarter. Now the raft became the sport of the elements—a toy in the hand of a lunatic; buffeted, spun, whirled, wrenched. There came a tremendous jerk as the cord that held the sea anchor snapped short. Judd's jacket disappeared in the blink of an eye, swallowed by the sea. Released from it's steadying pressure, the raft whirled instantly into a trough that yawned to receive it. For an immeasurable moment it lay there like an exhausted creature floundering to its death. Hills of black glass cradled it for the kill. Nothing seemed left of the whole universe but fury, darkness, clamor—and the doomed raft.

They saw a big wave rear out of the mist, moving down upon them. And the raft rose to meet its challenge as though on wings. Higher and higher the wave lifted, until it seemed to scrape the very clouds. Tranced, the boys watched that wall of water, stunned with a certainty of disaster. Its crest heaved over with a mighty sigh.

Down it smashed. The world ended. Out of chaos came the sound of splintering wood, weird as a scream in the night. The thought shot through Judd that the raft was being ripped asunder. And he himself was being pounded, slugged, gagged. His fingers loosed their grip. Then his whole body was jerked upward in space as the raft was flung into the air. It cartwheeled as it descended. Like crumbs from a shaken carpet the boys were catapulted into the sea.

Judd struck the water with breath-taking impact. Down, down he was shoved by a giant's hand. His lungs were squeezed to bursting. His head was blackness shot through with fiery pinwheels. . . . A heavy body raked his side with sandpaper. . . . Sharks. . . . Frantically he fought toward air and light. One thought only in his mind—Ken, who couldn't swim.

He shot up through blackness into twilight. His lungs exploded with cool draughts. Wildly he flung the sea out of his eyes, cast about. Conk was clutching the upturned raft, a terrible fear stamped upon his face. But neither Ken nor Terii was in sight. Ah, God—where were they?

A matter of seconds before Terii's head broke water, but to Judd an agonizing lifetime. Breasting the waves like a seal, the native clutched Ken's body in the crook of one arm, with the other striking out powerfully for the raft. Afterward Judd never remembered how he and Conk managed to right the raft. But somehow, by the grace of God and with the wind to help, they did right it. Then Terii and his limp burden were dragged to precarious safety.

They rolled Ken over, clung to his unconscious body with one hand, gripping the life lines with the other. The raft still was pitching too wildly to attempt more than to keep Ken from being washed back into the sea.

But already the storm, born of these unpredictable latitudes, gave indication of moderating as speedily as it had formed—as though in pity for their plight. The wind went whistling off into the empty spaces of the world; the cloud armada broke formation and sailed triumphantly away on the heels of victory. The sun came forth from hiding, final survivor in this battle between elements, and it fell upon tumbling wastes of water that were black in the hollows, fire-tipped on the peaks.

To Judd it seemed an eternity before he was able to turn his attention toward reviving Ken. No telling how much water he'd swallowed. A livid welt across one shoulder told where the raft had struck him. Ken's eyelids quivered, lifted slowly, as if weighted with lead. He stirred, attempted to speak.

"My glasses," he mumbled weakly. "Gone . . ."

"Take it easy, feller," Judd admonished. "What do you think you need glasses for anyhow?"

Ken's smile was sickly. "Guess I—tried to drink the —ocean——"

"Don't try it again, pal," said Conk huskily. "We'd miss all that water."

They were left shaky and unnerved by their terrifying experience; a forlorn-looking crew, water streamed from the clothing plastered to their bodies. Their eyes were red-rimmed and haggard. They hunched, trembling, in the reaction to their close call. Judd felt as if all his bones had turned to water; he marveled that he and Conk had been granted strength to right the overturned raft.

So unexpected was Terii's sudden shout that they started as if surprised from ambush. "Look, Americans!" and the native's voice climbed the scale. "The board—it is loose! The Sea God has come to our rescue!"

In overturning the raft, the great wave had splintered one end of the board which had defied them for so long. The whole plank had been wrenched free. Terii seized one end and gave a mighty heave. Up it came, at last. A six-inch spike protruded from a crack in one corner. With a whoop Terii yanked the spike free, fastened it to the cord that once had held his shark knife. "Aiá!" he breathed, his voice a thread of awe.

Judd's hands were unsteady as he attempted to rig the longed-for rudder. With remnants of the cord that had held the sea anchor he contrived an ingenious device that secured the plank firmly yet left the necessary play of free action. Awkward it might be, but the boy quickly demonstrated that by managing it as a sweep the raft would answer to command. Now, despite wind and wave, he could hold true to his course.

Their hearts were filled with gratitude, their spirits humbled; for they felt that with God's help their destiny was surely in their own hands. No longer were they forsaken upon the waters.

Chastened, they watched the sun burn its way into the sea, felt the dusk materializing from the league-long swells, saw Terii rise to his knees, head bowed, big hands clasped upon his breast. They understood that he was about to voice for them the gratitude in their hearts. Each one had helped himself over the toughest stretches with silent prayer. God had heard their petitions. Now it was fitting that He should be told their thanks.

Deep as the note of a conch shell Terii's voice boomed forth, forming the shape of Polynesian words strange to the ears of all save Judd Anders—the Lord's prayer:

> "*E to matou Metua i te ao ra,*
> *Ia raa to' oe ioa!*
> *Ia tae to' oe ra hao.*
> *Ia haapao hia ta' oe hinaaro*
> *Mai tei te ao Atoa na . . .*"

The timeless words, unintelligible as they were in this strange tongue, held a majestic rhythm that fell like a benediction upon those who listened. They bowed their heads in the darkness. And when Terii had brought the sonorous words to an end Judd added: "Let us pray, mates. . . ."

The deepest emotions of the heart are not easily expressed, and Judd Anders' lips were unaccustomed to voicing prayer. His young voice came husky with the great need to tell his gratitude and hope. "Watch over us, Almighty God. Help us to acquit ourselves like men. Make our hearts strong. And guide us safe to harbor . . ."

Conk's fingers touched the cross at his throat. "Amen . . ."

They felt better after that. The vigil of the night loomed less lonely. As they lay down to snatch what rest they could a profound thankfulness held them quiet, for no speech was needed to complete their unity.

Taking first watch, Judd hooked his arm over the rudder, felt the answering response of the raft. Low on the horizon Scorpio twinkled like friendly eyes, his lucky star—and under its glittering extremity he knew that the Solomon Islands lay waiting. His grip on the rudder tightened. . . .

Toward dawn, during Terii's watch, they were aroused by the native's excited cry. "Americans, listen well! Tell me what you hear!"

Instantly awake, the others strained for the source of sound which Terii's sharp ears had detected. Presently it reached them, scarcely to be believed: a whisper, a mighty sighing from across the waters. Nearer it ap-

proached, nearer still. It could have but one meaning.
Rain.

A ragged cry burst from swollen throats. Feverishly
the boys stripped off their salt-encrusted clothing,
doused it in the sea, wrung it out. Trembling, they held
themselves taut the better to listen, scarcely daring to
draw breath lest that God-sent whisper should vanish.
It strummed the night like aerial fingers drawn across
the strings of some heavenly harp. It came as the song of
a relieving regiment after a hopeless seige; and the
breath of it reached their nostrils long before the first
drops touched their aching flesh.

A brisk wind rushed in and the skies opened. Water,
sweet fresh water, came sheeting down. It struck with
the stinging force of a deluge, bounced upward from
the raft. It came in sheets to flatten the waves with its
weight. Those whose experience of rain is limited to
northern latitudes know nothing of the weight of water
released in a tropical downpour. Above the wild drum-
ming of the deluge the boys' incoherent shouts were
scarcely distinguishable.

Feverishly they allowed their rags to fill, then with
shaky hands wrung the fresh sweet water into their
throats. They lay with gaping mouths, felt blessed relief steal through desiccated tissue. The very air seemed
to have been washed clean by this water which washed
the brine from their bodies, revitalizing, cleansing them.
It soothed their aches, their sorenesses, their blisters. It re-

stored their souls. They felt that their troubles were over. They knew that they would live forever!

Even after the deluge, so short-lived, had passed on its mysterious way, the miracle of it lingered in their hearts.

And suddenly the clouds parted above their heads, revealing an unbelievable strip of stars.

CHAPTER VI The Submarine

WHILE SMALL FISH nibbled at the sea moss on the raft's undersurface Little Adolf proved particularly exasperating. He'd swim in close, roll just enough to expose his jaws in the tantalizing grin which by this time had set the boys' nerves on edge. More often he'd approach warily to windward, then shoot forward in head-on charge, only to swerve at the final second with a sinuous twist of his tail. Again he'd divert himself by diving beneath the raft, giving it a rude jolt in passing.

"Takin' us for a ride," Conk grated. "I'd like to bust him on the nose."

"I wouldn't advise it," Judd warned.

"Doggone, I can dream, can't I?"

More than once, as the shark cut sinuous capers, Terii's fingers sought the cord that once had held his shark knife. The six-inch spike which had taken its place would be a puny weapon against a shark, but the Polynesian fingered the spike and his eyes grew dark.

The rain of the night before, God-sent though it was, proved to be little more than an aggravation. As the sun climbed the tall sky thirst achieved exquisite torture; and so numb were their stomachs as no longer to seem a recognizable part of anatomy.

The strain was beginning to tell on nerves and tempers as well. They became irritable with one another, touchy over trifles which once would have caused them laughter. Shorter of speech now, each boy schooled himself to control before asking or granting any request. Subconsciously they recognized and resented the source of an irritability which had the power to disrupt their solidarity. Fortunately, when almost at snapping point, a sense of common danger reaffirmed their dependence upon one another, united them in the will to survive. At such moments they recalled the fate that Haru Osaka had so graphically painted for them, and some core of tough resistance snapped them out of despair.

That morning Little Adolf proved to be a turning point in their fortunes. Executing a quick turn at the raft's edge, the shark flipped up a bucket of water with its tail, while the wind caught the water and flung it full into Terii's face.

Instantly the native was on his feet. Anger blackened

his countenance. "Aiá, ma'o!" he shouted violently. "Devil of the sea! You wish to die?" Terii gripped the spike and sprang to the edge of the raft.

"Take it easy!" Judd cried in alarm.

But the native had flung caution to the winds. Before the others could restrain him he shot toward the water in a knifelike dive. At that precise moment Little Adolf came sweeping back toward the raft. Instantly Terii turned, shot up under his adversary. The shark rolled, jaws agape. But Terii's arm struck like a sledge, again and again. The spike plunged deep into the shark's gill—the only spot vulnerable to such a weapon.

Water foamed. A thrashing tail, Terii's drawn face. The powerful arm striking, striking. Red dyed the foam. Other sharks, lured by blood but chary of commotion, hovered on the fringe of battle, poised to dash in for the kill.

The boys stared, breathless. Consternation filled them. They could see that Little Adolf, mortally wounded, was slower in attack. The sweeping tail was sluggish. The jaws gaped, seeking to close on an enemy always just beyond reach. There was desperation now in Terii's face as he drove the weapon home.

Beating the water, the Polynesian maneuvered his victim close to the raft. But it seemed that life had not yet left the shark: a final swing of the powerful tail caught Terii full in the chest and knocked him under. But before Little Adolf could sound Judd had him by the gills, and the others helped to drag him aboard.

Terii's head broke water and he scrambled up out of danger.

The great fish was done for. As the last of life drained away a convulsive quiver ran the length of the once powerful body. And a shout of triumph ripped from Terii's throat—all savage now, forty generations of warriors crying in his blood.

Cutting through hide like uncured leather, with no implement sharper than a spike, proved a herculean labor. Deep holes were punctured in the tenderest part of the undersurface, and these were used as fingerholds to rip open the resistent hide. It was a bloody, exhausting business.

The shark's liver, packed with nutriment, proved unusually large. Judd divided it into equal quarters and passed it around. Ken gulped, but his squeamishness went down before the urgency of hunger, while Conk exhorted: "Wrap yourself around that liver, Professor. They feed the stuff to babies."

The meat proved strong and fibrous, hard going for mouths dry of saliva. They munched ravenously, not speaking. Separating the tough flesh from the hide proved difficult in the extreme, but hunger powered their hands. They ate as much as they could hold, ate until their stomachs rebelled; for they knew that the sun would rapidly spoil any meat not consumed. And when at last they could contain no more the remains of Little Adolf were flung into the sea.

"Now watch the Big League." Conk grinned.

The other sharks, hovering expectantly, surged forward like a pack of ravening wolves, fighting, tearing, rending.

With appetites appeased for the first time in almost a week, spirits aboard the raft soared high. Being set adrift seemed a thrilling adventure whose conclusion could only be triumphant! Terii was the hero of the day, albeit a modest one who wore his honors lightly.

But after the first fine optimism had worn away the gravity of this race against time drove home to Judd Anders. At an average speed of three knots, the boy figured they had covered some seventy miles per day, or roughly four hundred and thirty miles since being cast adrift. This was little more than half the distance which must be traversed if they were to reach the Solomon Islands before they turned into skeletons. The mysterious Ara Moana had served them faithfully, but who knew at what point the great ocean current might curve away on another tangent? The horrors that Haru Osaka had predicted loomed close. . . .

By this time the ritual of evening prayer had become a fixed part of each day's pattern, without which they would have lost hold on themselves. But it was torture to carry on through the hottest hours, and the lessons in navigation that Conk referred to as "bull sessions" were desultory, for concentration on any one subject grew increasingly difficult.

As hours merged into days and dragged away, they could recall into the limitless present only the faintest shadows of the past: the *Island Queen*, Haru Osaka, Karlson, Vana Vana itself—all were as unreal as the nautilus that drifted on the sluggish tide. Here they had always been.

Of them all Terii, conditioned by birth to the sun's violence, best withstood the days. Conversely he suffered more than the others in the chill of night. Ken too was holding out surprisingly well. But the flesh melted away from the framework of their bodies; they were all bones, all aches and sharp angles, while Conk's sunburn had developed into an acute condition. Wracked with fever, there were hours on end when Conk lingered at the edge of delirium, but he was indefatigably game. Within his wasted body a dauntless Irish spirit helped to carry him and the others over their darkest moments. They were aware that Conk's condition was far more serious than their own, and the fact that they were powerless to help him added to their misery.

There were moments when they all were lightheaded —heard sounds, saw objects which did not exist. That was why when, toward sunset of the tenth day, Terii insisted he heard a noise like the chug-chug of a motor, the others would not believe him. And a full hour passed before all agreed that there *was* such a sound—a burbling chug-chug-chug, like the exhaust of a motor launch.

Wild excitement surged through them.

"We're saved! We're saved!" Ken shouted, his voice unrecognizable.

They stripped off the remnants of their rags to hail whoever might be coming to their salvation.

Suddenly Judd gave a cry: "Look! What's that?"

Less than a quarter of a mile away, against the sun, a dark shape slid into the glittering path of light. They watched that shape in fascinated silence, scarce daring to believe it could be true.

"A tin fish," Conk croaked, lips twitching. "You guys—we're as good as rescued!" A demoniac frenzy possessed his bones. Wildly he waved his tattered shirt, shouting, imploring. Then they all were waving, yelling like creatures demented.

There was no answering response from the sub.

"Why don't they signal they've spotted us?" Ken groaned despairingly.

"They can't see us against this blasted sun glitter."

"They must, they've got to——"

The submarine was swinging on a slow tangent. Now the boys could make out her hull—a design unfamiliar and of monstrous proportions.

"What a whale!" Judd marveled. "But she's no Yank."

"Must be one of England's newest," Ken suggested hopefully.

The sub's crew, ant-small in the illusion of distance, raced across the deck. Now they were climbing into the conning hatch. Even as the boys watched, their hearts in their eyes, they knew that the hatch was being battened down. Obviously they had not been seen. The giant submarine was swinging away to westward, preparing to submerge. As her conning tower caught the full revealing brilliance of the sun Judd's breath gagged in his throat. For he beheld, painted in colors clearly visible, the emblem of the Rising Sun.

"*Jap!*" he whispered.

And they were all struck with consternation. The transition from wild joy, from the certainty of salvation to abject despair, had been so swift and overwhelming that their minds recoiled. What could it mean—this Japanese sub in British waters, in time of war, a thousand miles from any possible home base in the Carolines or Marshalls?

"Suppose they spot us now?" Conk muttered. "What'll we do?"

"We'll go overboard," Judd said grimly. "Let 'em have the raft."

Ken protested: "But we're Americans! Our country's not at war——"

"That didn't work with Osaka," the other reminded him. "Let's take a vote on it."

The result was unanimous. If the Jap lookout spotted them now they would go overboard. In the mind of each was the conviction that this giant sub meant them no good, that death would be preferable to capture.

Slowly, like some prehistoric marine mammal, the submarine slid beneath the surface of the sea. The chug-chug of its motors was muffled, silenced. Only a smell of burning fuel remained to persuade the boys that what they had seen could be actual and real. They knew the weak, breathless sensation of narrow escape.

After the submarine no untoward event flawed the passage of time. A profound lethargy settled upon body and spirit, taking cognizance only of daylight and dark. An occasional squall of rain slaked their thirst but brought a sharpened danger; for now little physical strength remained for fighting. Their morale, too, reached its lowest ebb. They felt that they must reach land soon or they would die.

Conversation was fitful, almost non-existent. It called for energy, precious strength to talk. They peered ahead through slitted red-rimmed eyes, seeking to pierce the secret of the horizon. But there were long periods when they were forced to keep their eyes closed against the intense strain of sun-shot water, which caused their vision to burn and blur, or summoned mirages that mocked them with false promise. Only the Ara Moana remained to hold out the vestige of a hope, for the current still swept onward in its mysterious course, still held true and undeviating.

But inevitably there came a day when they knew that body and spirit could bear no more, when the sea looked cool, and welcome, and inviting. . . . Deep down in those clear depths it seemed that they could see hands that beckoned, sea sirens who promised peace, rest. . . .

The same thought must have lurked in each boy's mind; for, glancing at their haggard faces, Judd Anders thought he saw the stamp of surrender. He could not blame them; the impulse was in his own heart too. But slowly he came to his knees, desperate in the need to rally their flagging spirits.

Dully they looked back at him, heard his hoarse voice saying: "Hang on, mates! Nothing can lick us except death itself. We've been two weeks with practically no food—but that hasn't licked us. We're going to make land or go to the bottom. *But we're not quitting!*"

"We're sticking, Skipper," Ken managed.

And though the other two had no words, Judd knew that he had won. Conk huddled, trying to protect his head with his blistered hands. Terii sat straight, scanning the horizon. As the raft topped a wave, hung for a second on the downward slide, the Polynesian said almost dreamily: "American, I see the green of trees."

Sharply Judd glanced at him, wondering if at last the native's reason had snapped. But calmly Terii reiterated: "It is green, like trees. American—it is land!"

Judd tried to stand, the better to see; but the weakness of his legs, the raft's motion threw him off balance. Ken helped to steady him, and the boy shaded his eyes against the glitter, scanning the horizon. He did not dare to believe. It was a cloud, a mirage.

But at the base of the cloud there was, indubitably, a line of green unlike that of the sea. Trees . . . green trees . . .

He gave a hoarse whoop, bringing the others to their knees.

The Submarine

"It *is* land!"

Ken let out his breath like an escape of steam. "And about time . . ."

They were all talking at once, stammering, incoherent. Was it really land? Were they being fooled again?

But with each passing moment it seemed that the cloud on the distant horizon took denser form and substance. It towered from the plane of the sea, filling their souls with wonder. Judd sculled while the others, flat on their bellies, paddled with feverish hands.

Throughout the hours of that interminable morning they inched toward land. Thirst forgotten, hunger too, their aches had miraculously vanished, for the moment at least. In their frenzy to win safety, salvation from the sea, they found themselves powered with a strength that, long afterward, they were to wonder at and marvel.

Then from far off came the first muffled roar and thunder of the reef: the booming surf smashing against the barrier coral. Sea birds were everywhere now, the sky alive with beating wings, with the clamor of hoarse cries. The island seemed like a magnet, drawing the raft inexorably forward.

Throughout childhood Judd Anders had watched natives bring their canoes through dangerous surf, had learned the trick himself. But a four-cornered raft was no surf boat, and the waves that were building from fifteen to twenty feet high pounded across the reef at terrific speed, foaming white and rich with a splendid wash far up the beach. It was as if the sea, in meeting the opposition of this impenetrable island, were flinging itself forward in all its tremendous power to smash, to shatter, to destroy.

Judd muttered: "We're in for a ducking," and licked dry lips. His hands were locked about the sweep. If only he could hold steady. . . .

His companions made no answer. Their hot eyes fastened on those building waves, tranced with a fearful fascination. They observed that the big combers charged one after another in groups of three, and that between these groups stretches of comparative calm were broken only by less dangerous waves.

The raft gained momentum. Whether they willed or not, those aboard it were now powerless to withdraw from a struggle that seemed certain to end in their destruction. The appalling thunder of the surf filled their ears; it was all about them, the very sound of doom. A wave rose behind the raft, scooped down upon it at tremendous speed.

"Hang on, all," Judd shouted hoarsely.

Out of a yawning hollow the raft rose like a gull to meet the base of the wave. Up, up they were swept. All about them was a scintillating boil of foam as they shot landward in a gale of speed. The wall of water passed under the raft, left it stranded as it thundered toward the land, smashed, and shot far up the beach.

Judd cast one backward glance. Behind him curled another wave, more monstrous than the first. He gripped the sweep till he ached with the strain, seeking to turn this insensate monster into a beast of burden. Again the raft replied to challenge, swept skyward on a cliff of water while the land rushed to meet it. But the backwash from the beach met the oncoming wave in a smashing cross-sea of conflict. Caught unfairly between the two, the raft upended and was hurled high.

Four boys were flung like pebbles into the shallows. Hammered, pounded, scraped, the breath beaten from their lungs. Eyes and mouths filled with sand. But above the chaos of that moment they knew the rake and bump of land.

Land . . . *Land!*

CHAPTER VII Jungle's Edge

AFTER SO MANY DAYS spent upon the water the earth heaved and billowed as the boys crawled ashore on a graceful curve of fine beach flanked by palms. Their legs felt numb and independent of their bodies, their pulses hammered with the effort of exertion.

Conk lurched forward, stumbled to his knees in the sand. A babble of incoherent sounds issued from his lips; his eyes burned with a fire of fever. Terii and Judd between them managed to lift the thin body, half dragging, half carrying it into the shade. As one who cares for a child, Terii's big gentle hands pressed a cracked coconut against Conk's fever-dry lips. As the cool sustaining liquid slipped down Conk's throat he swallowed convulsively, then with a sigh fell back, lapsed almost immediately into an unconsciousness which might have been sleep.

The belt of coconut trees that fringed the shore was backed by a dismal swamp of mangroves, beyond which the land rose in timbered slopes, tier upon tier, fading into a distance of lofty broken peaks misted with rain. Here was a forbidding and repellent land, the like of which no one of them had ever seen before.

"Do you suppose this is Guadalcanal?" Ken wondered, scarcely daring to believe.

Judd nodded as he sought to get his bearings, reconstructing in mind's eye a visual picture of Guadalcanal as he remembered its map. "That rounded hump to the south ought to be Vatupusau, some four thousand feet. And that peak yonder certainly looks like pictures of Mount Lammas—a good eight thousand."

"Yes, and that one in the middle could be Lion's Head," Ken agreed. "This is it all right, Skipper. You're some navigator!" And his eyes were bright with honest admiration.

- Terii discovered then that the sand was churned with footprints, while at the water's edge a long gash had been made by a boat's keel.

"Gosh, cannibals!" Ken breathed.

"Not unless cannibals have taken to wearing boots," Judd retorted. "A ship's crew filling water casks, most likely."

"The tracks look pretty fresh."

"Not later than this morning, I'd say."

The footprints led toward a stream near at hand that debouched sluggishly into the sea. And as the boys involuntarily followed with their eyes that maze of tracks a dead log on the stream's bank slid silently into the water.

"Crocodile!" Ken exclaimed. "You can bet these hills are full of surprises—unpleasant ones."

Little imagination was needed to picture all manner of living things—animal, reptile, vegetable, and human —concealed within that forbidding hinterland, and all potential enemies. The boys found themselves shivering in the moist heat as they lay under the palms, feeling the sting of returning circulation in their blood.

Presently Judd suggested: "We'd better scout for food. And Conk will have to be moved to drier ground. . . ."

It called for all their will power to overcome the inertia that reached into the marrow of their bones; but they were shamed into making the effort by the knowledge that they had been spared from the sea. They could not expire, effortlessly, upon this dismal strand.

Judd bent above Conk, saying urgently: "We're going to look for food, fella. We'll be back soon. You all right?"

A scarcely perceptible nod indicated that Conk understood.

Reassured, Judd turned toward the mangrove swamp, where a trail which might have been made by the hoofs of wild pigs led directly into a tangle of cane and reed and smothering convolvulus. The boy's legs wabbled unsteadily and he used a branch as a staff. Haltingly Ken and Terii trailed the leader, who moved deeper into the swamp, where the almost palpable smell of rotting vegetation, of decay and death, thickened and closed in upon them. Nettles tore at their suffering flesh; leeches fastened upon arm and leg, battened and dropped away, while mosquitoes attacked in stinging battalions against which there was no defense. But Judd shoved on ahead, his bare feet sinking deep into the ooze which seemed greedy to suck away his strength. A feeling of being in a mysterious, unnatural place smothered the boys like an enveloping blanket. As if the thought had been spoken and all emphatically had agreed on it, the idea fastened itself in each one's mind that the only thing to do was to put this malodorous swamp behind them as quickly as possible. Startlingly close at hand a voice screamed: "Look-you! Look-you! Look-you!" But it was only the voice of a jungle bird, so utterly human in pitch and timbre that it left them shaken and unsteady.

Presently the ground became drier as the path widened into a well-used trail through shoulder-high *sirio* grass. More cautiously now Judd advanced, every nerve alert, not knowing what he might be leading his companions into. With whir of wing a flock of hornbills gave ample notice of their presence; dragonflies with crimson wings filled the air. A sudden stealthy rustling among the leaves of a tree bespoke a monitor lizard, scuttling for safety. The boys could hear its claws rattling on the bark, but quickly it placed the tree trunk between its armored body and the intruders. Thirty feet above the ground it clung like some single monstrous survivor of an antedeluvian age. Spiders dangled from their webs—great black fellows with yellow spots and ruby eyes; the sticky threads of their webs brushed and clung to the boys' damp faces.

Unexpectedly the trail emerged into a cleared area where the grass had been beaten down—a clearing protected not only by the encircling jungle but by a close-woven ceiling of *oro* vines and creepers. In the center of this area they were astounded to behold a modern prefabricated structure. It was some forty or fifty feet square, a sight as unbelievable in that stretch of savage jungle as the Empire State Building would have been. Amazement struck them dumb. They stood without moving, as if they had struck down roots.

Finally Ken whispered: "Do I see what I think I see?"

Judd gulped, swallowed. "Doesn't seem to be anybody there. . . ."

Save for the high droning of insects, the clearing was locked within a spell of silence. There was no indication of human presence other than their own.

Gathering confidence, they edged forward. The building had been constructed of some synthetic metal, painted a dull mustard green. Walls and roof were mottled with a clever camouflage of daubs which art-fully simulated the dappling light and shade of vegeta-tion. The window openings were unglazed, but they had been screened. The single door boasted no lock. Judd eased up under one window, peered into the build-ing. What he beheld took his breath away.

Packing cases lined the walls. One or two had been partially opened, revealing cans of food. There was no one in the room. Motioning to his companions, the boy shoved open the door and entered. Lifting the lid of one case, he found it filled with rifles, of a short-stocked, long-barreled type unfamiliar to him. Other cases con-tained sidearms, rounds of ammunition, a machine gun and a 40-mm. cannon.

Picking up a can of food, Ken let out a low whistle. "Holy mackerel! Get a load of the label on this can!"

The others crowded close. The label, they saw, had been printed *half in Japanese.*

"Well I'll be . . ."

All the other cans were the same, good California tomatoes and peaches labeled with oriental characters. Medical supplies—medicines and bandages—products of a large American pharmaceutical house, likewise boasted Japanese inscriptions.

"This *can't* be Guadalcanal," Ken gasped weakly. "We've stumbled into one of the islands of the Jap Mandate."

"Don't be a fool! There are no Jap islands the size of this one. They're mostly atolls."

"Then what the . . . ?"

"Let's skip that for the present. We've got to get Conk here. The place is screened. There's food and medicine. If anyone shows up it's a regular arsenal and the jungle's at our back for cover."

"It's a natural," Ken agreed fervently. "Jeepers! There's even a stretcher to carry Conk!"

"Let's go!"

With grim determination Judd availed himself of a .45 and several rounds of ammunition; and with that compact fistful of blued steel his self-confidence went soaring. He knew that whenever a man has an even chance to fight back he forgets all about being scared. "Here, Ken, grab one of these things. May come in handy. You too, Terii."

Terii, however, had little comprehension of firearms. He chose instead a long-bladed bush knife shaped something like a samurai sword. Here was a weapon after his own heart.

So elated were they by their amazing discovery that fatigue seemed to have melted under the high pressure of excitement. Later they were to be caught in the backswing of nervous reaction, but at this moment they felt jubilant and strong.

By the time they returned to the beach they found that Conk had managed to prop himself against a palm. Though weak as a rag, he was in full possession of his faculties. At the triumphant return of his companions, however, the sight of firearms and bush knife, his jaw sagged foolishly, and he wondered if he were still a victim of delirium.

Quickly the others told him of the jungle clearing. "And we're moving into our new apartment right now," Judd finished.

"You're going to ride in state, Conk." Ken grinned.

"I don't need any stretcher! I got legs, ain't I?" Conk struggled to rise, fell back.

"Say, what do you think we ordered this limousine for? Come on, hop aboard."

With Judd at the stretcher's head, Terii at the foot, and Conk resigned to being carried, they again turned inland. Already the sun was sliding down the western sky; tropic night would be upon them before they knew it. To be overtaken by darkness while in the swamp would be, Judd felt, a calamity. For he doubted if Conk could survive a night's chill exposure to the mangroves.

Doggedly they drove their exhausted bodies; and it was with a flooding sense of last-minute reprieve that they again beheld the clearing, saw the camouflaged arsenal. And so unreal did it seem that they would scarcely have been surprised had it vanished into thin air during their absence.

Conk's jaw sagged with bewilderment as the boys set down the stretcher on a solid floor. He gazed about him wide-eyed, and his lips twitched as they fumbled for a quip: "Be it ever so humble, there's no place like . . ." But the words trailed, and he could say no more.

While Ken made use of canned heat to warm soup

Judd made a bed of blankets for Conk, forced him to drink some of the steaming liquid. Five minutes later he lapsed into deep sleep.

No one of them could have stood watch that night. They lay down with guns ready to hand, wrapped in Japanese army blankets, and fell instantly into dreamless slumber. Mosquitoes in thwarted billions droned against the screens, while tiny luminous beetles sparked and dimmed as they passed among the tree trunks. And the jungle clearing held its breath with listening as four boys, drugged with exhaustion, slept the night away.

The sun was an hour high when Judd opened his eyes. Instantly awake, he sprang to his feet, only to find that Terii was already preparing breakfast. Ken stirred, stretching cramped muscles. But Conk still lay quiet in his blankets, and it seemed that overnight his flesh had taken on a new transparency. A sense of foreboding welled up in Judd Anders which he sought to thrust away; but it clung to the edge of consciousness, stubborn as a burr.

They discovered that the only trail out of the clearing was the one by which they had entered. Elsewhere the jungle formed an impenetrable wall reinforced with nettle vine and dagger plant. With bush knives they set about clearing a path directly behind the house, leading into the heart of the forest. This would be their "out" when the Japs came.

"But we're going to stick right here until Conk's in shape to travel," Judd declared.

"Travel?" Ken echoed. "Where to?"

"How long do you think the Nips are going to let us enjoy their hospitality?" the other retorted impatiently. "I'm convinced this is Guadalcanal, but we've stumbled into a Jap hide-out and there may be others along the coast."

"But how could the Japs set up an outfit like this without the British getting wind of it?"

"Search me! But they're clever little devils and they move fast."

"Page Haru Osaka!" Ken murmured. "In the meantime I could make with a razor. I wonder if Japs don't shave?"

"They probably *pull* out the hair just to be tough." The other grinned.

Already Judd's thoughts were leaping ahead, laying plans for the inland journey he felt they would be forced to make. "We can't travel in these rags," he declared. "And we've got to have shoes."

"There's no clothing in these cases," Ken mourned. "Besides, I'll be darned if I'd wear a Jap uniform even if I could squeeze into one."

"That goes for me too. We'll have to rig up something out of blankets."

With safety pins and bits of string they lost no time making use of the gray cotton blankets. They achieved a sort of flapping drawers which tied about the ankles, and a tunic not unlike an abbreviated kimono—an ensemble that afforded them no end of amusement. Terii, the while, was skillfully plaiting Polynesian sandals for them all—stout soles of pandanus that could be bound about the ankles with vines.

They worked furiously against time; but three days passed before their grotesque but serviceable costumes were completed. With the .45s buckled in holsters about their waists, sandals bound on tightly, they burst into laughter, while even Conk revived sufficiently to wisecrack about what the well-dressed man would wear.

In Nipponese rucksacks Judd packed a few necessities he felt each one could carry. Before discarding forever the remnants of his former clothing, he salvaged the stub of pencil that had served him so long and well —the one object left which had the power to remind him of a world other than this incredible one into which he had blundered. He did not know that in the near future he was to need that pencil again. . . .

Rest, medicine, and nourishing food had worked their miracle with Conk McCoy. By the second afternoon he was able to sit up, even to take a few steps; and in silent gratitude the others watched his recovery, marveling at the reserves of force which sustained that thin body and gave it the will to go on. All gorged themselves on food and sleep. But there was a mark-time beat to the droning passage of the hours that stupefied them against their will, even as it warned them to beware. But not until the first legions of tree toads ushered in the evening with their shrill: "Cut it out; Cut it out!" did they dare to relax their vigilance. For at this hour it seemed that not even Japs would venture into the jungle.

This belief, however, nearly proved their undoing. It was the evening of their fourth day in the clearing. They had just finished rations when some prescience of warning more actual than a noise brought them to their feet. Stealing to the window, Judd peered across the clearing. The pit dropped right out of his stomach. Two short, bowlegged Japanese officers emerged from the screening trees, chatting nonchalantly. The boy thought, "This is it!" and flipped off the safety of his .45. Madly he motioned his companions toward the window at the back.

Terii and Ken swept up the rucksacks, ready against this emergency. With shaky hands Conk buckled on his automatic.

At that instant the Japs caught sight of the head against the screen. They sprang back into the trees. Sharp commands barked.

Judd cried: "Come on—*scram!*"

Four boys dove through the rear screen. They gained the jungle as the first volley of bullets ripped after them.

The chase was on.

During the next hours the Japs were seldom twenty paces away. The boys pressed forward through the gloom, lending Conk a hand wherever they could. Mud and creepers seemed to clutch at them with unshakable fingers, and they fought silently, desperately against these nameless enemies which felt for them, fumbled about their ankles, their legs, dragging them down, holding them back.

Behind them their pursuers were hacking at branches, and they heard the chattering bark of command. But they plodded on through the swamp, heads down, breath coming in gasps. Their thoughts, their very personalities became dissolved in the urgency of their struggle to escape. As they strove forward it seemed that the jungle itself was no less an enemy than the little yellow men who pursued them. The swampy water underfoot was growing deeper, deeper still. It seemed to Judd that he felt the slight tug of a current. As he passed unexpectedly out of the sheltering trees he sensed rather than saw that nothing was before him: an unknown river flowed there in darkness and he must lead the way across it.

Would it be shallow enough to wade? In a low tone he called to his companions, heard their reassuring replies. He moved out into the black and unknown stream. A scary sensation . . . Water icy cold against hot flesh . . . Creeping up his legs, his thighs . . . He held the .45 above his head but dared not shift the rucksack; he might have to swim. The water passed his hips, reached his chest, but he struggled forward. He didn't know whether he could swim if he had to.

The water shoaled and Judd clambered up out of the ooze, turned to lend a hand to his companions, discovered that Terii was carrying Conk on his back. A half hour of hard slogging brought them to higher, drier ground. With satisfaction Judd heard the grunts and exclamations of the Japs, who were still fighting their way through the mangroves.

"As scouts they're lousy," he thought. "They might as well wears bells."

After a few minutes of rest the boy passed the word to move more cautiously, and they again went forward into country that seemed more open. Now they were able to abandon Indian file and group more closely together. They fought against the feeling of complete exhaustion; they wanted sleep more than anything else in life. It was hard to breathe here. This wasn't air, Judd thought: it was a kind of pressure, a horrible pressure squeezing the air from his lungs. . . . His throat began to beat in giant throbs that merged with the sick pain in his head. A sudden stinging rake of nettle vine, full in the face, brought him to his knees, and he clawed his way on all fours, like some prognathous animal crawling away to die alone. He heard the sound of his companions' breathing, coming in ugly gasps; and that sound reached through to him in his extremity.

"Steady!" he called softly. "We're making it."

A break in the ceiling of the forest revealed a half-covered moon; its sickly light touched the shapes of vegetation that opened and closed like black, gargantuan fingers. A glimmer of phosphorescence emanated from patches of lichenlike fungus that clung to fallen trees.

The moon cleared suddenly and Judd saw revealed an open space of sirio grass, perhaps fifty yards wide, across which they must pass—fine targets for the yellow men so close now at their heels.

There was no alternative but to chance it. The very smell of defeat was in their nostrils. They huddled together as Judd explained the immediacy of their need. Conk was clinging to Terii's shoulder, his head sagging, knees half bent; but he rallied at Judd's urgent voice, stood swaying but unsupported. He brushed his hands across his eyes, as if to free himself of a spell that still bemused him.

"Can you make it, Conk?" Judd whispered. And felt the other stiffen to meet the challenge, heard him say, "Let's go, pal."

Ahead, the clearing gleamed palely. Behind, the Japs were hacking through trees not ten yards away. Judd broke cover, dashed blindly into the open. Conk sped at his shoulder. Terii, Ken—they were somewhere. . . . Judd dared not glance back. There was only that wall of trees, safety, to be reached.

A volley of shot ripped after them. A groan—but Judd kept running. The whine of bullets everywhere.

Four boys gained the cover of the jungle. Three of them whipped about, guns drawn, ready to mow down the first Jap who crossed that area of moonlight. But it seemed that the enemy had no intention of playing clay pigeon. Perhaps too he was chary of being lured farther from his base. In any event no attempt was made to cross that open space in pursuit of four boys who had discovered and rifled a secret arsenal. After what seemed an interminable time of waiting the staccato of Jap voices could be heard—in retreat.

Then silence, immediate and uncanny, gripped the jungle. In panic Judd remembered the groan he'd heard. Whipping about, he discovered Conk outstretched on the damp ground. Moonlight, pale and spectral, shafted down upon the form so strangely quiet. Swiftly Judd knelt, slipped an arm beneath the other's shoulders, and at his touch a deep quivering sigh explored the length of Conk's body. A sticky warmth pulsed against Judd's bare arm. He probed for the wound, found it, knew sickly that it was hopeless. There was nothing anyone could do for Conk now. This was a catastrophe beyond the reach of human skill.

"Quick, Terii—Ken! Some dry leaves, anything. He —he can't lie here in the mud——"

Through the darkness Judd could feel rather than see Conk's eyes fastened upon him; and he knew that in those eyes there would be a look of final acceptance, as if what had happened in the end must have been implicit in the beginning.

"How're you feeling, fella?" Judd's voice came husky.

Conk swallowed—a ghost of his old-time chuckle. "Boy, I feel like . . . an eight ball in a side pocket. . . ."

After that he was silent. They could only make him

as comfortable as possible. Nearly at the end of his physical endurance, Judd fought down the rising threat of rebellious nerves and knew that with his strength ebbing he was almost at the mercy of that threat. Desperately the boy reminded himself that upon him alone devolved the necessity for steadiness and clear thinking, and he must not fail. He must not fail. Presently he felt quieter, managed to say: "You—you want anything, Conk?"

"Sure . . ." Whisper-faint came the reply. "A . . . frosted chocolate . . . lots of ice . . ." As if he were dreaming there in a pool of blood, Conk continued to lie quietly on his back. Under the spectral moonlight the winglike murmur of the casuarina trees was the whispered rise of his fate. . . .

Stressed against the torrent of their feelings, the others huddled close to the recumbent figure, as if they would bring Conk warmth, comfort, reassurance.

"Hold on, Conk. Just a little longer . . ." Judd's voice came muffled and unsteady. "Hold on, fella. . . ."

"Okay, pal. . . . I'll try. . . ." Those were the last words that Conk ever spoke. His blue eyes lived on stubbornly in the feverish mask of his face; the light in them was slow to dim, as if a wick were being turned gradually down. Soon there would be no more light. . . .

Stooping, Judd's fingers sought the boy's wrist. The pulse was still, the flesh already growing cool. The heart that had beat so indomitably had come to final rest.

Under the whispering casuarina trees Terii set about digging a shallow grave with his bush knife. And when it was all over, and the ground had been heaped back and covered with a tangle of liana, Judd lifted Conk's gold cross and rosary; his lips fumbled for the shape of words. He knew no formal prayer for such a moment. He could only ask God to watch out for Conk, to help him over; and the words came now from the bottom of his heart.

"Watch out for him, Lord. He's only a little guy. Take care of him. . . ."

Now three boys, not daring to retrace their steps, turned their backs on the lonely grave and plunged deeper into the unknown jungle.

Hours later, when they paused to snatch an hour of rest, Judd discovered that the gold cross and rosary still were clutched in the grip of his fist.

CHAPTER VIII Ambush

SOME OCCULT malicious power seemed to have designed the jungle to be the natural enemy of man. Danger permeated the air, an almost palpable force, imbued with a quality of being alive in a tangle of hairy vegetation. Orchids, exotically beautiful, breathed out an unsuspected poison; a harmless-looking branch could quicken to life in the swift striking of a snake. Great black bunches of fruit hanging from the trees were, in reality, flying foxes hanging head downward. Here was a presto-chango land whose surprises were always charged with peril.

Doggedly the three boys fought their way to higher ground, away from the fever-haunted swamps. Terii led the way, slashing with his knife at nettle vine and liana. Now and again they emerged into open spaces which were never wholly level; and they came to dread these clearings where razor-sharp ledges gashed their feet and concealment was impossible. Almost they welcomed again the protective cover of the jungle, for here at least was safety of a kind.

Or was there? They could not have told at what moment they first became aware of being shadowed. It was as if beneath their consciousness some prescience of danger were warning them to beware.

When Judd called a rest they huddled together in a moment of precarious silence, some nameless caution impelling them to mute their voices to whispers.

"It's the natives this time," Judd muttered.

"How do you know?"

"I don't . . . but Japs would be sending bullets after us by now."

"If it's the blacks," Ken protested, "why don't they let fly an arrow?"

"Don't ask for it, screwball!"

It was Terii who made the first tangible discovery. Well in the lead, he jerked to a sudden halt and sprang back. "Aiá!" he gasped, awe-struck and trembling, his face a mask of horror.

The others peered into that malignant wall of trees, seeking to pierce its dangers. Confronting them on the trail, a pair of skulls had been placed at eye level in the crotch of a stick; primitive, anthropoid, yet indubitably human skulls. The flesh had long since dropped from the bones, but portions of the scalp with woolly hair adhering showed them to be skulls of Melanesians. On one a tomahawk gash over the left ear bit deeply into the brain cavity; on the other a small round hole in the forehead and a larger one at the back showed where the bullet had made its entrance and exit. In each case death must have been from ambush and instantaneous.

"Aué!" And now Terii's voice came as a thread of superstition and horror.

They speculated on the meaning of this warning, if such it might be, and discovered that the skulls marked a fork in the trail. To the left a leafy tunnel rose toward higher ground, straight inland. To the right—there was no telling. Was it good sense to continue on either of those trails? Wouldn't it be wiser to shun them both and strike off in a fresh direction?

Ken settled the matter. "We've already been spotted. If they're laying for us we haven't a Chinaman's chance of giving them the slip. Might as well stick to the trail and bluff it out."

Judd agreed. "We can't expect to cross this devilish island without running into natives," he said. "We'd better learn how to handle 'em."

"All the Solomon Island tribes are not cannibal," stated the ethnologist.

"We'd be slim pickings anyway," the other came back at him. "They'd have to fatten us up, and that part wouldn't be so bad!"

But Terii's face was grave as he scanned the faces of his friends. The human skulls, come upon so unexpectedly, had shaken him as no actual physical threat could have done. Here was a superstition that reached backward into the misty beginnings of his race, perpetuated in tales told around the evening fires. However, Judd was confident that, whatever decision he and Ken might make, the Polynesian would abide by it blindly.

He gave Terii a reassuring clap on the back, and it was Judd who this time took the lead, circling around the grisly skulls, breathing more freely when these gruesome objects had been left behind. In the mud footprints could be seen, prints of bare feet so small they could have been made by children. Off to the right Judd thought he saw a shadow shape, scarcely human, dart through the trees. He snapped to a halt. In the center of the trail, leaning toward him, a spear had been driven like a challenge. The point of human bone, wickedly barbed, gleamed with dull lights.

Almost at once a shrill voice cried out of nowhere, in pidgin: "Stop trail! Make talk!"

Back to back, the boys stood at bay, weapons held in readiness.

"Come out!" Judd shouted, his voice tense. "Make talk!"

They waited—every faculty, every fixed gaze thrusting ahead, seeking to penetrate the lurking threat of that screen of trees. A minute of silence thundered to eternity. The entire universe began to drum monstrously. They had the crazy notion of having dreamed the skulls, the spear, the voice. . . . The dreadful feeling of waiting for a blow to fall increased degree by degree, unbearably. And then a figure took form out of shadow—a man scarcely four feet six inches tall. His miniature dark brown body was almost naked save for a G string and a flamboyant headdress of feathers and shell. A bow of black palmwood and half a dozen arrows bristled in the pygmy's hand.

The little figure struck his chest a drumlike blow. "Me Kongu!" he shrilled. "What name b'long you?"

Judd signaled his companions to lay their weapons on the ground, a command they obeyed reluctantly. Then toward the pygmy the boy outstretched one hand, palm up, and answered: "Me friend, Kongu! Me 'Merican."

Ken whispered: "You'd better prove it. Give him a present."

A present . . . Judd tried to think which of his hodgepodge belongings might make a suitable gift. In a flash of inspiration he extended Conk's gold cross and rosary at arm's length. The pygmy's smoky eyes glistened as they fixed upon this treasure.

"Present b'long you," Judd cried. "Take!"

Desire for possession was slow to overcome generations of wariness. A long moment stretched before the pygmy laid down bow and arrows, edged gingerly forward, poised for instant flight. At the same moment a score of naked brown little figures sprang from leaf and branch, arrows drawn, covering their leader's advance— a wild and savage band that outnumbered the boys seven to one.

"This is it!" Ken breathed. "Why'd we ever lay down our guns? We can't pick 'em up now without starting something."

Judd made a show of confidence he was far from feeling, took another step toward the little savage. Light caught and glistened on the gold cross. With a motion so quick as to baffle the eye Kongu's hand darted forth to seize the rosary. Clutching it like an excited child, he sprang backward to the protection of his warriors. They crowded round their leader, chattering like chimpanzees, while the rosary passed from hand to hand. Gold, it appeared, was a metal beyond their understanding, its yellow brightness a marvel out of the white man's world of mystery.

When Kongu again glanced at the boys it was evident that this gift had turned the trick. His betel-stained mouth cracked into a grin that was like the gaping of an unhealed wound. "You-fella stop house b'long Kongu!" he cried. "Me friend 'Melican. No friend Jap!"

"What name Jap?" Judd threw out quickly. Lord, what did this savage know about Japs?

"Too-much no good," the pygmy retorted. "Make fight along white-fella. Kill 'im dead-finish."

This statement threw the boys into a pitch of excitement. Was Kongu trying to inform them in *bêche-de-mer* that Great Britain was at war with the Japanese?

"What else could he mean?" Judd demanded. "How could this little devil even know what a Jap was?"

"Perhaps he knows about the hide-out on the coast," Ken suggested.

"I doubt it. These tribes stick pretty close to their own territory."

"Shall we take a chance and go to his village?"

"You'll go on foot, Professor, or be carried on poles as a nice fresh corpse," Judd promised. "All we can do is keep our fingers crossed."

"It's been a long time since these blacks were cannibals."

"Yeah. As long ago as last week!"

Kongu settled the matter with a peremptory command. "We go!" Imperiously he motioned the boys ahead of him with a gesture which left them no choice.

Judd assented, stooped to retrieve his .45. But Kongu's voice cracked like a whip: "No! No take gun!"

Judd straightened, his mouth grim. "I reckon we play ball with the little man."

"It's tough to be bumped off with your own gun," Ken complained.

"Perhaps you'd prefer an arrow, Professor. Come on —we'd better do as he says."

Without further protest the three boys swung into line. Instantly several of the little warriors darted in, seized the two automatics and Terii's bush knife, then sped on ahead, disappeared from sight. Defenseless now, there was nothing for the boys to do but advance. Kongu marched beside them, more amiable now that they had proven themselves amenable to persuasion.

Judd tried to draw more information about the Japs, but Kongu only reiterated: "Jap 'e fight. Kill 'im dead-finish."

Presently they came to a swift-running stream that leaped over black boulders alive with millipedes. The banks were steep cut and to Judd it looked as if they were in for a good ducking; but almost at once he discovered a catwalk of rattan spanning the stream. Already the pygmies were darting across this fragile bridge; beneath Judd's and Ken's greater weight, however, it sagged dangerously, but held. Terii's great bulk threatened to sweep him into the rushing torrent. By the time the big Polynesian had gained the opposite bank and hauled himself to safety he was panting with relief.

"That bridgework was designed for midgets, not giants," Judd kidded him.

During the next hours, weary though they were, Kongu permitted them to halt only once to drink from the natural water supply secreted within the green trunks of bamboo thickets. The pygmies dextrously tapped sections of stem, motioned the boys to drink before the water escaped. Many sections of the thicket had been already tapped, indicating that this was a favorite drinking place of the savages, one of whom produced a bunch of blood-red bananas whose insides proved to be as soft as strawberry ice.

Kongu explained: "Banana b'long time before white man 'e no come yet."

An hour later they stumbled upon the village without forewarning, suddenly, as all things seemed to happen in this unpredictable jungle. A high stockade of thorn and dagger plant enclosed a score of wattled houses perched off the ground on stilts. The surrounding jungle grew close to the stockade walls, its branches and creepers almost forming a roof to lock away this miniature world from the sight and knowledge of men.

As the band of pygmies and their three captives slid through the narrow opening a pack of snarling, verminous dogs set up a pandemonium, while the potbellied children who had rushed to welcome their fathers fled screaming with fright at sight of the white strangers.

Ken murmured: "I bet these people tell their kids that the white man will get 'em if they don't watch out."

Tiny ageless women, curious as monkeys, peered with bright eyes from the shadowed gloom of the thatch. Kongu proudly led the way through the village, where at the far end a high-peaked abode of imposing dimensions proclaimed itself the *tambu* house of the men.

"This must be mine host's hangout," Ken observed.

"Pretty keen," the other agreed. "He's the big shot around here all right."

A notched log led to a platform several feet off the ground. Climbing it, the boys found themselves in a dim cool structure whose openwork bamboo walls permitted an unhampered passage of air. The rafters were blackened with smoke, through which row upon row of pigs' jawbones glimmered dimly, reminders of many a feast, while here and there a human skull stared down at the newcomers out of black, sightless sockets. Whether these were skulls of departed warriors or trophies of the hunt remained problematical. The latter seemed more likely, since several of the skulls were larger than pygmy size. In racks along the walls were dozens of spears, elaborately carved and cruelly barbed with bones from the wings of the flying fox.

"What name this village?" Judd demanded of the little chief.

"Name Valé-Munga," came the proud reply.

"Ask him what he's done with our guns," Ken whispered.

At the word "gun" Kongu's eyes sparked. "Me friend b'long white-fella," he asserted.

"He talks too darn much about friendship," Ken grumbled. "I wish he'd do something to prove it."

As if in understanding of this complaint the little chief clapped his hands sharply. In response to this command two youths appeared, bearing calabashes of boiled pudding, a third brought a gourd of stagnant water, while a fourth produced a basket of small green bananas.

"Time b'long *kai-kai*," said Kongu, urging them to eat.

"Just express a wish," Judd chuckled.

"Maybe it's poisoned." Ken eyed the meal dubiously.

"Maybe it isn't. Anyway, here goes!" Squatting on the floor beside the calabash, Judd dipped his hand into a gray, mucilaginous substance not unlike the two-finger *poi* of Hawaii. Gingerly he tasted it. "Sago," he decided, "not half bad."

Ken tried it, pulled a sour face. "Tastes like billposter paste to me!"

But Terii fell upon it with gusto, his huge hand scooping up such quantities that the calabash soon had to be replenished, and the astounded pygmies crouched around the Polynesian, their eyes never leaving the great bronze body. To these little savages in their minia-ture world Terii was a veritable giant who could have held any one of them in the palm of his hand. They dis-cussed his powerful physique, the cast of his features, his manner of eating, switched their attention to con-sider the white boys—and all in an unremitting clatter of chitchat.

"Sounds like an afternoon in the primate house." Ken grinned. "What in heck do you suppose they find to talk about? You'd think they didn't see each other every day."

"This place ought to be an ethnologist's dream," Judd said.

Earnestly the other agreed. "I'd give my left arm to stay here and write this up!"

"Your left arm? Say, stop asking for trouble, will you?"

"They must have had plenty of contact with white men," Ken mused, "because they speak pidgin. But Terii certainly has them stymied. They haven't taken their eyes off him."

Judd chuckled. "They're probably trying to decide how he'll taste best—baked, broiled, or roasted."

The pygmies' confusion was clarified by Kongu. Pointing a bony finger at the big Polynesian, the chief cried suddenly: "What name, what name? You-fella all-same Jap?"

Taken aback by the preposterous question, Judd and Ken burst into laughter, while Terii joined them in a mirth which rocked the rafters. The pygmies stared back at their captives, round-eyed and puzzled.

"Him no-fella Jap," Judd laughed. "Him-fella fight Jap kill 'im dead-finish quick!"

Here was the reassurance the little chief had been hoping for. He huddled in conversation with his warriors, then, turning to Judd, he asked, slyly: "You savvy number one master live mountain b'long him? Talk-talk 'Melican?"

Judd struggled with the meaning of these words. "Do I know a big chief who lives on the mountain and speaks 'Merican? Is that it?"

Kongu nodded animatedly. "Talk-talk 'Melican!"

"He's coming here?" Judd demanded, bewildered.

A vigorous denial. "No! Mebbe you go number one master bimeby."

"Where is he?"

Airily the pygmy swept an arm in the direction of Guadalcanal's mighty ranges, indicating that the mysterious chief might live anywhere within a radius of several thousand square miles. "Mountain all-same b'long him," he said.

"You take us there?" Would this be the chance to cross the mountains and reach the British-held coast and safety?

But Kongu grew crafty. "Me go talk-talk number one master. Bimeby short-time mebbe he say you come."

It occurred to Judd that if this mysterious chief could talk "'Melican" he could read it too. "You'll take a message to him?" the boy demanded.

Kongu's eyes were blank; a written message lay beyond his comprehension. Quickly the boy tore a strip of bark from the wall; from the rucksack produced his stub of pencil—barely enough left to grip.

Printing carefully in bold letters, Judd wrote: "Three Americans. Friends. Help us." And to Ken he added, "Shall I sign my name?"

"Not unless you've got friends in these hills, Skipper."

Kongu tucked the message into his bark belt, made a motion to indicate the sun's passage across the sky. "Sun

'e come up I go," he said. "Time b'long sleep now!" and
forthwith rolled himself in his grass mats.

"Meaning which?" Ken speculated.

"That come daybreak the little man will hit the trail
for number one master's. Maybe we'll be invited later
if we're good boys. In the meantime I can use a little
shut-eye myself."

"You and me both!"

The beds were merely ragged pandanus leaves spread
upon a corrugated floor, being laid in a line down each
side of the tambu house. The feet of Kongu's warriors
almost met in the middle. Between the sleepers a small
wood fire smoked and glowed. Already the windowlike
doorway had been barricaded from the inside, that no
one might leave or enter before daybreak. Above each
warrior's head his battle-ax and wicker shield had been
placed instantly to hand.

Weary in every limb and sinew, the boys sank down
on the mats. But exhausted though they were, their
nerves had been strung too high by events of the day
for sleep to come easily. They thought of how narrowly
they had escaped falling into the hands of the Japanese.
They thought of Conk lying alone under the casuarina
trees, and their hearts constricted. The precariousness
of their present situation, outwardly pleasant enough,
came driving home to them and its gravity was not to be
denied. They had escaped the Japanese only to become
prisoners of the pygmies—captives in a savage stronghold, surrounded by warriors who dozed with battle-

axes at their side. How, Judd asked himself, would they escape? Where could they escape *to?*

Ken shifted in vain attempt to make himself comfortable on a floor corrugated by bamboo poles. A profound sigh escaped him. "The raft was a Beautyrest mattress compared to this," he murmured. Nevertheless, he was the first to fall asleep.

For a little while Judd and Terii continued to converse in low tones. The Polynesian spoke in native tongue of matters that disturbed him. "American, I do not like the smell of these black eaters of men! There is no good in their hearts."

"We'll find out tomorrow maybe."

"I believe they mean us harm," the other persisted.

"They've had plenty of time to kill us," Judd reminded him.

"True. . . . Still, I do not like the smell of them." With which Terii rolled over and was instantly asleep.

But Judd lay wakeful. All around him in shapes scarcely less dark than the night itself the pygmies breathed stertorously in troubled sleep, as if nameless fears stalked their dreams. And suddenly the strangeness of this moment passed over the boy—the blind fortuity of chance which had led him to this incredible place, where millions of brassy-throated tree toads seemed to be shrilling: "Cut it out! Cut it out!"; where flying foxes swooped above the thatch with a swish of membraned wings; where the melancholy note of the nightjar sounded deep within the jungle.

Who was this mysterious number one master? Was he Melanesian, a pygmy? Or—was he a Jap? The Japs might offer Kongu a fine reward for capturing the three Americans who had discovered their hide-out. Why not? Why not? . . .

Not until the hour before dawn did Judd Anders fall into an exhausted, troubled slumber.

Kongu and his warriors were making ready for their mountain journey.

Judd demanded: "How long till we hear from number one master?"

The pygmy shrugged, a movement that set the feathers of his headdress dancing. "Long-time little bit mebbe. Short-time little bit mebbe," came the cryptic answer.

The boy groaned. "Anywhere from three days to six months!"

Before departing, Kongu introduced his son—a tiny well-knit youth of sixteen with an alert face, and bearing the name Fintimbus. Kongu indicated that Fintimbus was to be the boys' servant during the chief's absence. But Judd understood that a guard was being appointed to keep an eye on the American captives.

This suspicion was quickly confirmed; from the moment of the chief's departure Fintimbus never left the side of his charges. They were allowed to roam at will within the stockade walls but were angrily barred from passing through the gate. A glimpse of the warriors who guarded the single entrance with wickedly barbed spears quickly dissuaded the boys from forcing the issue.

Judd soon became restive under this confinement, but Ken's only regret seemed to be lack of camera, note-book, fountain pen, and calipers—the trappings of his profession. "What a break to get a scoop like this," the ethnologist bemoaned, "and not be able to do a darn thing about it."

"Heck, if you ever get back to Chicago you can tell 'em what it was like," Judd consoled him.

But Ken shook a sorrowful head. "They'd never be-lieve me. They'd say I was just another 'inspirational' scientist."

With boundless enthusiasm, all ethnologist now, Ken poked into ways and customs, examined artifacts, imple-ments, and idols with impartial interest. Within this stockade he found a people who had been living throughout dynasties of human history: a high-spirited community barely emerged from Stone Age develop-ment, whose life from cradle to grave was a battle against enemy forces—hunger, disease, hereditary foes, poisonous reptile, insect, and plant. Yet however dif-ficult the struggle for survival, they remained the happy possessors of a gift for laughter. It never failed to aston-ish the Americans to hear mirth of such rich proportions issue from such lilliputian bodies. The source and cause of that laughter often was incomprehensible, but its effect was none the less contagious, sweeping the stock-

ade like fire through a field of sirio grass. This happy
trait went a long way toward reassuring Judd Anders,
for it was difficult to believe that a laughing people
could be a treacherous foe.

Men, women, and children were addicted to use of
the betel nut, which stained their mouths crimson,
blackened their teeth, augmented their natural physical
ugliness. Even small children were allowed to smoke
villainous cigarettes of some pungent black leaf.
Matches were non-existent, but as fires continually
smoldered in each house, the natives seldom were compelled to resort to the traditional method of fire making
with sticks.

Almost completely naked, the pygmies strove to
make up for their lack of natural comeliness by a wealth
of fantastic decoration—headdress, nose plug, earring,
and bracelet. Through the pierced septums of their
noses they thrust the tails of pigs, bone plugs, or quills.
From holes drilled in the flange of a nostril wisps of
feather or grass nodded jauntily. The headdresses were
elaborate arrangements of feathers and orchids, or
sprays of glittering green beads which, upon closer in-
spection, resolved themselves into green beetles. This
resplendent attire was reserved for the men and boys of
the tribe; women and girls, being considered less important in the social scale, must content themselves with
bracelets of trochus shell.

This enforced sojourn in the pygmy village proved
an excellent opportunity for the boys to brush up on

pidgin, Fintimbus being a willing tutor. Judd had forgotten how much fun it could be—that amazing conglomeration of English, French, and Portuguese words, the *bêche-de-mer* of Melanesia, first introduced by sandalwood traders and blackbirders. Combinations of words were odd and unsuspected. "What name?" meant why or how. A stomach-ache became "Belly b'long me walk about too much." Any woman was a "Mary," a child a "pickaninny." Oddly enough the word "kill" meant merely to strike. It took "Kill 'im dead-finish" to mean slay!

By means of this extraordinary lingo planters could issue orders to their laborers, missionaries were able to exhort their flocks; while British, French, and Orientals, knowing nothing of one another's language, were able to converse freely in pidgin.

One evening at dusk the boys were permitted to watch the snaring of the flying foxes which came over the village at first dark. But they were cautioned not to stand too close because, as Fintimbus explained: "Too much smell white man. Fox 'e no like no come!" The nets were marvelously woven of black fiber, some thirty yards long and sixty broad, slung on high poles above the flaming coral trees. Cunningly concealed ropes and weights held the nets in the treetops. As the flying foxes swept in to feast on the coral flowers the nets were let go with a crash. Down to earth came the foxes, tasty morsels for the soup pot.

But diverting as these interludes proved, Judd's impatience turned to anxiety as three days elapsed without Kongu's return. The conviction grew upon the boy that the mysterious number one master, with whom the pygmy chief had gone to bargain, was none other than a Son of Nippon who would make short work of them all.

At sunset of the fourth day of waiting a pygmy warrior came running into the compound, bearing news which set the women busy at the cook fires, caused the children to vanish into the jungle in search of fruit. Excitement rippled through the village like wind through a field of cane, setting the women a-chatter as they kneaded sago into cakes for baking.

An hour later Kongu himself appeared with his men, stamping impressively as he passed through the gate of the stockade. Unable to contain himself any longer, Judd hurried to greet the little chief.

"What name?" he demanded. "What say number one master?"

Kongu eyed him with bright, dancing glance. "Number one master say you-fella come talk-talk 'Melican!"

Caught between relief and apprehension, Judd asked: "When do we start?"

Kongu's arm simulated the sun's course. "Short-time little bit."

"Tomorrow?"

The little savage nodded, spat a crimson flood of betel. "Time b'long eat now!" he said. "Tomorrow—number one master!"

CHAPTER IX Number One Master

ROUSED FROM SLEEP while it was still dark, the three boys followed Kongu and his band across the compound, slipped through the stockade and plunged into the obscurity of the jungle trail. They felt cold and empty-bellied, scarcely rested. Kongu had returned to them their guns, and this was the one bright spot of dawn; for it seemed unlikely that they were being led into ambush fully armed.

Rain was falling steadily. Moisture dripped and oozed from every leaf and twig; the dank mustiness of centuries of rotting vegetation closed in upon them like an enveloping fungoid growth.

Kongu and Fintimbus led the way, bare feet sinking

noiselessly as shadows into the spongy trail. Judd and his companions followed in Indian file, at their backs a half-dozen pygmies bristling with spears and arrows. The way led up and up, toward drier ground, skirting dead-end chasms at whose unimagined depths water could be heard gurgling and churning. Monstrous crevasses where one unwary step would have spelled oblivion were overlaid with vine and creeper and were undiscernible except to the eye of a savage. Another facet of Guadalcanal was revealing itself, scarcely less terrible than the mangrove swamps of the lowlands.

Presently the pygmy chieftain enjoined his followers to silence, suggesting that the territory of another and hostile tribe was being entered. At unfortunate moments when Judd or Ken snapped a twig, the pygmies grimaced at them furiously. At one point Kongu left the path entirely, cutting a circuitous route through the bush until, some miles farther on, they again emerged upon the trail.

At midday, on the edge of a vast savanna of waving sirio grass, they halted just long enough to snatch a mouthful of food and quench their thirst. The splendid savanna shimmered in wind and sun, extending as far as the eye could reach: an inland sea of grass. High above and beyond, the serrated peaks of Lion's Head could be glimpsed through a wreath of cloud—seemingly as unattainable as a mirage. To Judd it was incredible that he and his companions would ever gain those heights, cross over the backbone of this formidable island, and drop down on the other side.

"Lord," he breathed. "If this island could only be tamed and put to work! I wonder if Great Britain realizes what she's got?"

"She's welcome to it!" Ken exploded, clawing at a leech that had fastened itself between his shoulder blades.

Terii likewise, with his expanse of exposed flesh, was being made miserable by the insect pests of this devil's country, so unlike his beloved Samoa.

The strain of this forced climb was beginning to take its toll of Ken's strength, but doggedly he kept pace, while Kongu and his warriors seemed to move on hidden springs, resilient and inexhaustible. The pygmies resumed their chatter presently, indicating that hostile territory had been by-passed. Here the air was clearer and thinner, more tonic and invigorating, while a buzzing in Judd's ears bespoke a higher level of altitude. Now the earth was rocky and substantial underfoot, and the boys felt their spirits lifting as the gloomy lowlands were left farther and farther behind.

"Where stop?" Judd demanded.

Kongu answered airily: "Long-time little bit."

Ken groaned, his knees sagged. "That means from two to ten miles! I'm fed up with this long-way short-time stuff. Do you figure we're in for a night in the jungle?"

"Could be."

For the first time Ken himself voiced the thought that had been been plaguing Judd. "You think this little guy is on the square, don't you, Skipper? What's to prevent him from leading us straight into a trap?"

"He's had plenty of chance to polish us off if he wanted to."

"I know," the other grudged. "But this darned number one master doesn't sound so good. Have you thought that Kongu might be taking us to Jap headquarters?"

"I've thought of that."

Attempting to follow the drift of the boys' words, Kongu grinned amiably as he isolated the word "Jap." "Too-much bad kind!" he stated, eyes dancing. "Me kill 'im dead-finish!"

"Kongu," said Ken earnestly, "if you're not on the level I swear I'll lose my faith in human nature."

"You'll lose more than that!" Judd retorted.

"Long-time little bit now." Kongu nodded vigorously, motioning toward the heights of the mountain. "Number one master 'e stop." And from a note of excitement in the pygmy's voice the boys suspected that at last they might actually be approaching the high chief's domain; involuntarily they felt a rising excitement within themselves.

But it was late afternoon before, wading a chill mountain stream, they emerged quite unexpectedly into a clearing and beheld a house: a long bamboo structure with a thatch of nipa and a deep-shaded piazza. It trailed a group of outbuildings, from one of which a curl of smoke rose skyward.

Kongu cried: "House b'long number one master!"

and almost pranced across the clearing, shouting a gibberish as he advanced.

"So this is it," Judd said. "Where's the master himself?"

Even as he spoke a big man moved from the shade of the piazza—a white man deeply burned by the sun. And there came to their ears the unmistakable half-Cockney twang of Australia. "Well I'll be blowed!" the big man bellowed. "Fancy meetin' you 'ere, you sweeps!"

Judd's knees went weak. A gasp broke from Ken. The big figure advancing to greet them was none other than Clydebank, that ace of the British Colonial Intelligence—better known to the boys as Red Malloy. Two years ago Malloy had contributed to the excitement of their adventures at Vana Vana, but they had never expected to clap an eye on the man again. Now here he was on this mountaintop in Guadalcanal—the same masterful egoist with that intangible quality like the sharpness of flint, the toughness of oak.

Dressed in shorts and singlet, a battered topi cocked on one side of his head, the rangy grace of Red Malloy's movements belied fifty years of rugged living. An irregular scar from right cheekbone to a corner of his mouth lent him a rakish look, while his bright greenish eyes took in everything at once.

Judd managed to stammer: "Dr. Livingstone, I presume?"

Malloy gave vent to his remembered chortle—that deep rumble which suggested he was having a good time inside himself. "Looks like you Sydney-side millionaires have been takin' another yachtin' trip. Welcome to Guadal, my merry lads. It's the Devil's own caldron you've jumped into this time."

"You're telling us?" Ken demanded weakly.

Already Malloy was herding them toward the cool gloom of the piazza, where to their amazement they discovered chairs, deep-cushioned and comfortable, a table all set for dining—civilized appurtenances such as they had not seen for many a long day. The big Australian clapped his hands to summon his black boy, Atamat, at the same time shooing Kongu and Fintimbus toward the outbuildings in the rear.

"We can talk and eat at the same time," the man boomed, motioning the boys toward the table, where four places had been laid. Malloy had been expecting guests, all right.

"I could eat half a steer," Judd sighed, sinking wearily into a chair. He thought he had prepared himself to face any possible contingency—Japanese officer or head-hunting cannibal. But meeting up with Red Malloy on this remote mountaintop flooded the boy with a sense of relief that momentarily left him weak at the knees. He could only sit and stare foolishly at the big Australian, shake his head with wonderment, and stare again.

Terii, ill at ease on a European chair, squatted on the mats Polynesian fashion, eying the platters of food which black Atamat was producing. White men could always talk, talk, talk. It was more necessary to eat!

Malloy's first statement rocked the boys on their heels. "I suppose you lads don't know that your country is at war with Japan?"

"We thought it might be England," they stammered.

"England too. Looks like you've got a few current events to brush up on." And briefly he sketched for them the treachery of Pearl Harbor and its immediate aftermath.

Ken interrupted to say: "So that's what Osaka meant about December seventh going down in history. The little ringtail knew it all the time!"

Malloy wagged his head. "Blimy, what bloody fools we've been, and 'ow we're goin' to pay for it! But tell me—where'd you coves drop in from? Blast me if you don't turn up like a bad tuppence."

Judd recounted the events which led up to being cast ashore on Guadalcanal.

At mention of Einar Karlson's name Malloy of the Colonial Intelligence gave vent to a loud groan. "Blimy, what I'd give to get my 'ooks into that bleeder!"

"You know him?"

"Know 'im? 'E's number one Nazi agent on the Brisb'n list. And Uncle Sam's been combin' the Pacific coast for 'im."

Judd said: "He certainly slipped a fast one over on the New Zealand Intelligence. They swallowed his line —bait, hook, and sinker."

Red Malloy snorted. "Just like that New Zealand outfit. They'd let a whale slip through a sieve." He turned his head to bellow: "Atamat, y' black limb! Fill up those plates. Look alive, y' fat fraud you!"

Eyes popping, the black boy jumped to obey. Alternately browbeating and spoiling his servants, Malloy enjoyed a worshipful obedience from them all.

The man shoved back his plate, settled his rangy frame in a low chair, and swung a leg over the arm. With the air of a monarch bestowing a favor upon a vassal, he accepted a gourd which Atamat filled with heady brew, drank deep, wiped his mouth with a swipe of the forearm. As Malloy surveyed his unexpected guests his eyes missed nothing of their makeshift clothing, assorted bruises, cuts, scatches, stings, and swellings. He chuckled with wry amusement.

"A ruddy mess you lads 'ave got yourselves into this time," he mused. "Guadalcanal was thought up by the Devil 'imself when 'e didn't 'ave nothin' more pressin' to attend to."

"It's not exactly friendly," Judd agreed, rubbing his bumps ruefully.

"Friendly? Blast me! Your gun will rust while you're reachin' for the grease. Leather mildews, rots before your eyes. You'll pick up dhobie itch, athlete's foot, and prickly heat. There's water everywhere, but thirst will drive you crazy. And this blasted jungle water carries typhoid, dysentery, cholera, and undulant fever. You go to bed soaked to the skin and so blinkin' cold you're a good prospect for the undertaker. As for these jungle birds—don't mention 'em in my presence. There's one that sounds like a dog barking, another makes noises like a man banging blocks of wood together; and still another that moans like a woman bein' slowly murdered in the dark! The crocodiles and wild hogs won't bother you—much. But the little creatures who depend on you for a livin' don't wait to be bothered: those angels of the mosquito family for example—Anopheles, Aëdes, and Culex. These little sunbeams bring you yellow fever, dengue, malaria, and filariasis."

"Are you working for the Chamber of Commerce?" Ken interrupted.

"Mind you," the other persisted, "I've said nothin' abaht the ticks, sand flies, fleas, and lice—not to mention the leech. You'll get very attached to *'im!* E's abaht an inch long when empty, but 'e can penetrate two thicknesses of cloth to get at you. Your only satisfaction is applyin' the coal of a cigarette and watchin' 'im pop off."

"Can't you find a good word for the place?" Judd wanted to know.

Malloy took another swig from the gourd, surveyed his guests quizzically. "Well, there's the little matter of poisoned arrows and spears, deadfalls and witchcraft. No! Guadalcanal's not the place to bring your aunt Addie. But"—and his green eyes twinkled—"I love the blinkin' 'ole!" He shouted suddenly, "Atamat! Fill up those plates before I blow y'r ruddy 'ead off!"

The boys gorged on the first good food they'd known in weeks, while the big Australian kept up a running commentary of talk. The roast pig was followed by honey parrots, a delicious savory dish; and then a portion of grilled flying fox, as tasty as pheasant. All this was topped off with "millionaire salad"—an extravagant dish whose preparation involved the destruction of a palm, since the salad was made from the tree's heart.

Feeling that he'd burst on another mouthful, Judd finally shoved his plate aside. "But you haven't told us what in thunder *you* are doing on this mountaintop, Malloy. What's this number one master stuff? Still the supersleuth, tracking down spies?"

Malloy's eyes sparked. "Somethin' like that," he confessed. "When war broke out with Germany in '39 no one expected these islands to be in the war zone. But three days after Pearl Harbor the Japs occupied the northern Gilberts. The fat was in the fire for certain. We knew then that Australia was next on Tojo's schedule."

At that point Judd broke in excitedly to tell about the Japanese hide-out on the coast.

Malloy nodded thoughtfully. "Sounds to me like Kukai Point—a likely spot. We've uncovered half a dozen such arsenals, and God knows 'ow many more are 'idden on a thousand miles of coast line. The blasted little Nips 'ave been sneakin' supplies in to secret bases, where they can menace convoys bound for Australia. If they succeed in gettin' Tulagi Harbor we'll 'ave our 'ands full."

"But what's your special assignment?" Judd persisted. "Or is it a state secret?"

The other grunted. "Seein' as we've been deep-dyed conspirators before, I can tell you some of it. There are six of us district officers who've set up an Intelligence center in the bush. Friendly tribes like Kongu's help to keep us posted. I have my own teleradio outfit, but the native grapevine is mostly as speedy as radio and not bothered by static. For example, even before Kongu 'imself came to inform me I knew that two white men and a brown one had been captured in the jungle and taken to Valé-Munga. Naturally I didn't suspect it was you."

"But how in heck . . . ?"

"Don't ask me 'ow they do it," the other came back at him. "I'd like to know myself. It's as if the trees themselves could talk and the stones pass on secrets. Of course the gong language of the drums explains part of it. You can 'ear the bloody things for miles and miles, sendin' all manner o' messages." The man chuckled. "I 'ad a pretty good hunch from the way you printed that note that you weren't a Jap. But there was a chance you might be a Jerry. In that case Kongu 'ad 'is orders and I don't doubt there'd 'ave been a merry feast in Valé-Munga."

The boys were astounded by the fact that Guadalcanal, all but unknown, should so swiftly have moved into the forefront of world significance.

"How do you plan to repel a Jap invasion?" Judd

wanted to know. "You've no fortifications, no troops——"

"Right, my bucko. But we 'aven't been entirely idle. That's been part of my assignment—trainin' bands of friendly natives as scouts and guerrillas. Naturally these blacks couldn't fight well-equipped Nips on equal terms. But you can't beat 'em as bushfighters. Fuzzywuzzy commandos, I call 'em. They'll keep everything under control till the Yank Marines can get 'ere."

"Our Marines," Judd shouted excitedly, "they're on their way?"

"They'll be landin' in Brisb'n one o' these days," the Australian assured him, "and Guadalcanal's only a spit and a jump away. That's one thing abaht Uncle Sam—you can always count on the old boy in a pinch. It'll be tough for Tojo when the Yanks arrive."

"Gosh," Judd breathed, eyes shining, "I'd give my eyeteeth to be with 'em!"

"You and me both," Ken threw in.

"Ai!" Terii cried, thumping his broad chest. "Samoan is American too. I be Marine!" And he broke into makeshift pidgin. "Shoot Jap, kill 'im dead-finish no good kind!"

Malloy roared, slapped his thigh a mighty wallop. "The war's as good as won," he shouted. "But it's a bloomin' long swim from 'ere to Australia. 'Ave you thought of that?"

"Where's the interisland service?" Judd demanded. "Can't we get a boat?"

The man shook a gloomy head. "Guadalcanal's practically cut off from the outside world. The fact is, I've picked up rumors of a giant Jap sub operatin' from a secret base. She's been sinkin' merchant vessels, interferin' with outside help."

A whistle escaped Judd. "A giant sub?" he exploded. "I'll bet we've seen the one you mean!" And he broke into the tale of the mysterious Japanese submarine which had almost run down the raft. As his words tumbled over themselves Red Malloy's eyes darkened and the twist of his lips grew bitter.

"The ringtails 'ave thought of everything," the man acknowledged savagely. "No Jap's good till 'e's been dead three days!"

"Tojo's been planning this for thirty years," Judd reminded him.

Sourly Malloy agreed. "You Yanks 'ave a word for it: we're gluttons for punishment."

An idea that had been formulating in Judd's brain took shape and conviction. His eyes were steady with purpose as he said: "Malloy, you've got to help us get to Australia. Somehow! Yank Marines are landing there and we're joining the scrap."

The big Australian looked at the boy who faced him so squarely, and something at the back of the green eyes kindled. "The Three Musketeers, eh?"

"You'll help us?"

"In every way I can!" The man's face grew thoughtful. "My friend Bill Boyd down at Wanderer's Bay will rent you his ketch. That part's easy. It's gettin' down to the coast that's another story! Trouble's brewin' in these 'ills that 'asn't got nothin' to do with the Japs."

Impatiently the other demanded: "What sort of trouble?"

"The usual. Langalis and Ringapats—the bad boys of the 'ill tribes. Traditional enemies. Eat each other whenever they can. You'll 'ear their drums tonight back-talkin' at each other."

"Their quarrel isn't with us. Can't you find a guide to take us through their territory?"

"I might be able to bulldoze a guide for you," the other returned cautiously, "but the blighter wouldn't stick if you ran into trouble."

Judd's determination remained unshaken. "We'll have to take that chance."

Red Malloy did his best to paint a gloomy picture: these crazy-headed kids would not go off half cocked if he could help it. "You'll 'ave to travel light and live off the country. You'll 'ave only what you can pack on your own shoulders, and believe me it's easier to march barefoot in this country than it is to travel on an empty paunch."

"I'm counting on you, Malloy."

The man made a further attempt at dissuasion. "The next twenty-five miles is a limestone barrier of canyons, fissures, and crevasses. No water—not a ruddy thing to eat but the *goru* palm, and the rock pythons are so 'ungry they practically knock you down."

"How do you know?" the boy countered.

"Because I've been there, you dinkum little idiot!" Malloy blustered.

The other came back at him triumphantly. "Then I reckon we can make it too!"

Malloy banged the table with his fist. "But I've never been beyond the village of the Ringapats!" he shouted. "The Langali country is almost unknown. Not 'alf a dozen white men 'ave seen it—and come out alive to talk abaht it."

His words fell on ears that were deaf. The man sighed, capitulated. "I might 'ave known I was wastin' my breath. . . ."

"Then you *will* find a guide?"

"There's a black devil in the next village," Malloy said heavily, "a Ringapat who married outside his tribe. 'E knows the country like the back of 'is black 'and. Maybe I can bully 'im into it."

Atamat was summoned. Orders were issued for half a dozen men to seek out the Ringapat and fetch him to Red Malloy, hog-tied if necessary. "And mind, y' black rogue," Malloy finished darkly, "I'll blow y'r bleedin' 'ead off if you show up 'ere without that Ringapat. Look alive now!"

"Couldn't we bribe Kongu to guide us?" Ken suggested.

Malloy snorted. "No pygmy would tackle the Langali country, not if you flayed 'im alive."

"What stirred up the Langalis this time?"

"Well, it's like this. No one's ever supposed to die a natural death in Guadalcanal. Poison or witchcraft are held to be the real reasons, and such a death demands revenge. The Langali chief died last week—old age like as not. But Ringapat witchcraft gets the blame. The Langalis are out for blood—anybody's blood. Head-huntin' is still the pay back in this part of the world. With nothin' else to interest 'em, nature gave these black devils a savage heart to keep the tribe alive."

The man broke off and came impatiently to his feet. Now that the die was cast there was no time to be wasted. "We'll be gettin' your gear assembled," he said. "I don't doubt that ruddy guide will be 'ere in the morning. As to clothes . . ." He cocked an eye, guffawed with laughter. "Blimy, what a parcel o' Marines you'd make in those diapers! You look like Omar the tentmaker's kid brother. We'll rifle the slop chest for new togs."

Dungarees, shirts, sun helmets, and boots. First-aid kit, firearms, and maps. The remainder of the day was spent in assembling gear. Only on the matter of shoes for Terii did Red Malloy come a cropper. "We don't get many giants to outfit in these parts," he explained, "mostly pygmies." The man chose only those foods which combined a maximum of nutrition with a minimum of weight: bouillon cubes, powdered chocolate, tea, iron ration, and vitamins. "You can eat goru palm for bulk," he told them, "and that's abaht all the blasted stuff *is* good for."

The slop chest yielded a tent fly of oiled silk that folded up to handkerchief dimensions; and as a final gift the man presented Judd with a cigarette lighter guaranteed to function in rain or wind.

"And now one last thing before you turn in," the man said. "Y'r spot o' quinine!"

Malloy lined them all up for their first preventive dose of this lifesaving drug. "Nar then, nar then, open y'r mouths like little men! Malaria kills off more white men in one year than the cannibals do in fifty. Over Rabaul way they got a song, goes like this:

> " '*When the top of your 'ead*
> *Seems as if it would crack,*
>
> '*And you think there's a weight*
> *Of a ton on your back,*
>
> '*When you chatter with cold*
> *Though your skin's burnin' 'ot,*
>
> '*And you're feelin' like 'ell,*
> *Then it's certain you've got*
>
> '*A rousin' good dose of*
> *Mala-a-a-aria!*' "

There, that ought to tide you over a day or two. . . . And now to bed, my merry lads. Mornin' will roll around before you know it."

They gripped hands, and beneath the surface raillery of the Australian's words the boys sensed a deep and genuine concern for their safety. It touched them more than they could have told; and they knew that, anxious though they were to be on their way, they'd say good-by with reluctance to this bluff, boisterous, generous, kindly friend.

As for Judd Anders, his thoughts were already leaping ahead, hurdling the dangerous miles. In his mind's eye he saw the shining coast line of Australia, alluring as a mirage in the desert and somehow miraculously attained; and he saw his own enlistment in the Marines, Ken and Terii still with him. . . .

Ken dug him in the ribs, laughed: "Still crystal-gazing, Skipper? Snap out of the trance! What's on your mind?"

The other relaxed, laughed back. "I was thinking that if we can't square accounts with Haru Osaka one way we'll do it another!"

"The Marines have landed, eh? Come along, let's get some shut-eye. Good night, Malloy—I'll remember you in my prayers! You're not worried about us?"

"Not 'alf!" came the scoffing answer. "I figger you were all born to be 'anged!"

CHAPTER X The Breath of Danger

TEN HOURS of dreamless sleep found the boys refreshed, eager for the first round of the perilous journey across the backbone of Guadalcanal.

The arrival of the Ringapat guide momentarily dampened their enthusiasm, for he was a surly-looking savage who obviously had been rounded up with difficulty. He owned but one eye, shifty and restless, the other having been gouged in some bloody encounter; chevronlike scars ornamented his face, while his hair had been bleached by lime to a dull rust, and his naked black hide was scrofulous.

Judd Anders' heart sank as he knew that his fortunes were to be bound up with such an ill-found specimen.

Malloy's face was a mirror of distaste. "What name you?" he demanded.

"Me Sul," came the gruff reply.

"Sul, eh? What a name, what a name! You savvy country Ringapat, Langali?"

"Savvy, master. Too-much no good kind."

"I ain't askin' your opinion. You guide white-fella master, eh?"

With his one eye the Ringapat cast a supercilious glance at the three boys. The cringing servility of his manner toward Malloy fluctuated toward arrogance. "Too-much bad walk about b'long bush," he said haughtily. "Me fright too-much."

Malloy hooted with derision. "What name you fright?" he cried roughly. "You all-same fella Mary, eh? You guide white-fella master or I'll skin your bloody 'ide off!"

The Ringapat, obviously anticipating the threat to be put into immediate effect, capitulated sullenly. "Me guide," he whined.

"That's better," the Australian thundered. "Get along now till you're wanted."

As the Ringapat moved off toward the outbuildings Red Malloy shook his head dubiously. " 'E's ugly-shaped enough, God knows. The spit o' the Devil. There's an axiom in this country—the darker the 'ide, the darker the 'eart. Still, 'andsome is as 'andsome does. I don't know where to look for another."

"You think he'll stick with us?" Judd queried uncertainly.

"You can drop me a line and let me know," came the pointed rejoinder. "All I can say is, you've been attended by the good luck that goes with fools and children, else you'd 'ave been dead fifty times over. I'm 'opin' your luck still 'olds!"

But with the optimism of his nineteen years Judd's spirits were not dashed for long, and the big Australian tried his best to match that youthful zest. Superintending the packing of the rucksacks, issuing commands to his blacks, the man was everywhere present.

In their new outfits of dungarees and khaki shirts the boys felt strange to themselves—so long they had worn makeshift rags. They surveyed one another with admiration and amusement.

"Will you be needing the limousine this evening, Mr. Van Astor?" Ken asked toploftily. "Or shall I tell Parker to bring around the town car?"

Red Malloy chortled. "'Ere's something I bloomin' near forgot, and worth all the rest of your gear." He produced what appeared to be two firecrackers wrapped in oiled silk.

"Dynamite?" Judd queried.

"Not 'alf! Rockets."

"What name rockets?"

The man grinned. "Keep 'em for fourth of July if you want to. Just don't let 'em get wet."

"But . . . ?"

"A rocket saved my life once in the Ringapat country," the man explained grimly. "Might do the same for you. Now one last piece of advice and I'm done. Don't trust Sul any farther than you can throw a bull by the tail. 'E'll probably see you through, but if 'e shouldn't —don't get rattled. Just keep your eye on this compass I'm givin' you, and remember that Wanderer's Bay is due sou'-sou'east. Better get goin' now, lads. . . . You've a bit of walkin' to do before you even smell the country of the Ringapats—and blimy, 'ow they do smell!"

Kongu and Fintimbus shoved forward to bid the boys good-by. As Judd looked down into their dark faces, so filled with gaiety and high spirits, it seemed incredible that once he could have suspected them of treachery.

Almost wistfully the pygmy chief asked: "You savvy come back short-time little bit mebbe?"

Judd pumped the small black hand. "P'raps long-time come back mebbe," he promised.

A final handshake, a parting word from Malloy: "Tell the Yanks I'm holdin' off Hirohito till they get 'ere. But tell 'em to 'urry!"

"We'll be seeing you," Judd promised, gripping the man's big paw, and the boy's heart swelled with gratitude. "No use trying to say thanks, Malloy, but——"

"Whist and stow your jaw!" came the gruff reply. "Get along now or you'll miss the boat." Malloy looked about for Sul. "Where's that Ringapat? Fire and damnation! *Where is he?*"

Sul appeared, taking his time, walking haughtily as he

passed through the ranks of the blacks. A long-bladed bush knife was thrust through his bark belt; a net bag containing his "possibles" was slung across one shoulder. A six-foot bow of black palmwood and half a dozen arrows were his weapons. Without deigning to offer the boys a glance he led the way up the rocky heights behind the clearing.

At the summit the boys turned for a last glimpse of their friend, saw the big Australian surrounded by his worshipful blacks. They did not know that this was the last time they were to see Red Malloy.

Ahead of them the mountain barrier was sharply defined against the sunrise; while far below the grassy savanna was filled with milky cloud whose wraithlike vapors drifted above a thousand square miles of forested range. The immediate way led through slabs of rock that rang with a hollow sound of iron beneath the boys' hobnailed boots. Passing over the high divide, climbing, slipping, struggling for a foothold, they gazed down upon a breath-taking world of tormented shapes —peaks, fissures, erosions—the terrible limestone barrier against which Malloy had warned them. It was indeed a terrible expanse of land, silent and void of life; and involuntarily they tightened their muscles, as if to meet a challenge. Honeycombed with craters, sharp-edged as shattered glass, every step must be watched and fought for. A stunted tangle of growth was broken here and there by the wretched goru palm.

Toward the southeast they wound their way, past

shadowy caves in whose dark depths the ghostly drip-drip of falling stalactites could be heard, while now and again came the murmur of an underground stream moving sluggishly at the earth's core.

At an altitude of seven thousand feet a rainy mist chilled the boys to the bone. Adding to their discomfort, the small fern leech attached itself in thousands to their faces; and so numb was their skin that not until they felt a tendency to blink were they aware of the little black worms working themselves under the eyelids.

With each passing mile Sul became more exasperating. So laggard was his pace that the boys constantly trampled on his heels, while the expedient of sending him a hundred yards ahead resulted only in overtaking him quickly. Judd tried the plan of going ahead with Ken, leaving Terii to keep a watchful eye on the savage. But Sul's gait now became so slow that the boys were compelled to wait until he caught up.

Judd reprimanded him sharply. "What name you! Too-much no good kind!"

But the Ringapat only cast him a venomous look and showed no indication of mending his ways.

That first night Judd parceled out the rations with a sparing hand. Sul kept to himself at his own cook fire, and the boys welcomed this respite from his hateful presence. Since there was no way of knowing how long they would be on the trail, all were agreed to reduce the meals to absolute minimum. There was always the goru palm, but they cast a scornful eye at this insipid water-logged vegetable which filled the stomach with bulk but not with nutriment. How little they guessed that, days later, goru "cabbage" would be welcome indeed!

That night they hugged the fire, caught their drinking water from the rain that trickled off the canvas, brewed it into piping-hot tea. But the wind struck at them with knifelike edge. They dozed fitfully, were glad to be up and on their way again by first light.

Moving laboriously, south-southeast by the compass, they plodded through a nightmare region where the outlook never changed. And it was at this juncture that they had their first misadventure. Sul had lagged so far behind as to be out of sight; Judd and Ken in the lead heard a hoarse shout behind them, turned in time to see Terii preparing to swing his bush knife at a rock python of tremendous size. The snake, thoroughly aroused, was making straight toward the native, and even across the intervening distance Judd could hear the hissing that issued from the wide-open jaws. The blade flashed in Terii's hands—a true blow that caught the python behind the head. The great reptile paused for a split second, as if dazed, then kept coming. Terii retreated a step, gripped the knife firmly with both hands. This time the blade swung home, nearly severing the spade-shaped head from the body. The undulating coils went limp.

Panting, Terii stared down at the python, then with

one foot kicked furiously at the limp body. The next second he let out a mighty yell; for some involuntary muscular reaction had caused the dead snake's tail to coil about the native's leg. The other two boys were forced to use their bush knives to pry it loose. A dark welt on Terii's flesh quickly became a painful swelling.

"Aiá! What a devil's country is this one!" the Polynesian gasped, wiping cold sweat from his brow. "I have no liking for this land!" Aboard the raft he had challenged shark and storm, but a monster such as this he had never even imagined.

Almost imperceptibly the air grew softer, the wind less chill as a change took place in the nature of the country. Crevasses and craters gave way to timber—small growth at first. At lower altitudes the forest would again become jungle as the boys moved into the country of the Ringapats. But with all its hidden dangers the jungle in prospect seemed less formidable than this inhospitable region they were leaving behind.

That morning, for the first time, Judd experienced the listlessness which heralded the symptoms of malarial fever. In spite of quinine, he was in for his first bout with the dread malady. Wrathfully he cursed the malarial parasites multiplying by billions in his blood stream, and wondered if possibly Sul's laggard pace were not best suited to this devilish country. His head began to pound with sick rhythm, and he could feel the fires of fever licking at the edges of consciousness; but he made no mention of it to his companions.

They came upon a shallow, rust-colored stream, marking the first belt of jungle, and paused on the near bank, waiting for Sul to catch up with them. When the savage arrived he motioned across the stream and said curtly: "Land b'long Ringapat!"

The territory of the Ringapats . . . As Judd plunged into the stream the water felt icy cold against his feverish skin. Mosquitoes were so thick as to be a humming mist in the air and he fought them desperately but without hope. They were in his nostrils, his ears, his eyes; they settled on wet clothing that steamed in the heat. And whenever afterward, in years to come, Judd Anders thought back to the country of the Ringapats, he remembered that smothering mist of mosquitoes that blinded the sight and gagged every drawn breath.

As the boy pushed his way into the forest it became apparent that the Ringapats had deliberately wrecked the path. Numerous mighty trees had been felled across the trail and everywhere nettle vines had been allowed to grow unchecked. In some places dagger plant had been so pruned that it leaned shoulder-high over the path, retarding progress.

Sul hung back nervously, starting at shadows. He was impervious to reprimand. When the boys stopped to snatch a moment of rest and a cigarette the savage sat apart from them in sullen silence. He rolled his own cigarette of native leaf, inserted it in the end of his bamboo pipe, and for some reason refused the offer of Judd's cigarette lighter. Certainly the Ringapat was capable of producing his own fire, which he did quickly enough. From the net bag came a small hard stick, split at the end; this Sul gripped with his feet. Then, using a strip of rattan like a string around a drill, the shavings in the cleft of the stick took fire by friction. A matter of seconds—the fire was there! This action seemed to restore something of the Ringapat's overweening self-confidence. He cast a supercilious glance at the cigarette lighter. Out of his own superior wisdom he had created fire.

Controlling a rising exasperation, Judd demanded: "Where stop village b'long Ringapat?"

Haughtily the savage condescended. "Long-way little bit."

At which response Ken groaned aloud. "That means from three to twenty miles. This guy has no sense of time or distance. No sense at all, in fact."

But Judd was wondering what sort of reception they would receive in the village of these notorious Melanesians. The British had never succeeded in winning them over, or the Langalis, for that matter. Instances of treachery toward strangers who entered this terra incognita were too numerous to be thought about with equanimity.

They came to a place where the track radiated in five directions, like the spread fingers of a hand. Near by the gardens of the Ringapats lay neglected, choked with weed and overgrown with nettle. So swiftly does the encroaching jungle take over that it was impossible to guess how long these cultivations of yam and taro had lain untended by their owners. Sul declared that the central path led into the village proper, and the boys stepped warily along it, suspecting ambush at every turn. But the silence was primeval and unbroken.

Presently they came upon Tintogomo—the mountain village of the Ringapats: fourscore nipa houses straddling a long gloomy alley that was shadowed by dark overhanging trees and faintly illuminated by the fires of a dying sun. No sound of human voice, of barking dog, of squealing pig. The village was void of life. There were only the empty houses and the hideous idols that guarded them, locked within the mesmerism of some unbreakable spell. And the boys edged forward, quivering with expectancy, ready to defend themselves at an instant's need.

In a loud tone Judd called out: "Hallo-o! Hallo-o-o-o!" His voice fell into the green void like a stone flung into a pool; and diminishing ripples of sound disappeared into the encircling trees.

They singled out the tambu house of the men and warily entered. It was empty. No weapons, no mats, no implements of any sort. Each house in turn proved to be the same. Desertion of the village must have been hastily determined and carried out. A bit of sago left in a calabash had not yet been entirely devoured by rats. It was Terii who came upon the dead body of an old, old man. Too decrepit to flee, the ancient had been abandoned to die when an entire population with all its personal effects had moved deeper into the jungle to escape its enemies. The silence seemed tingling and alive with ghostly overtones of the voices which so recently had sounded there.

There was a touch of awe in Judd's words as he said: "Looks like they decided to bolt in a hurry."

"I've counted eighty houses," Ken put in. "That means five or six hundred people. The Langalis must be bad medicine if they can scare off a village of this size."

"Right!" the other agreed. "And with males outnumbering women as they do in the Solomons, that'd leave some four hundred fighting men."

"Say, I hope we don't have to go to the mat with the Langalis."

"You take the words right out of my mouth."

They rigged their tent fly in the shadow of the tambu house, while Terii built up a fire and set about preparing their evening meal. Sul, consumed by some secret anger, refused to share the boys' fire, built one of his own, and turned his back upon them. Earlier in the afternoon the savage had managed to catch a cuscus, a small possumlike animal. This he had been carrying with its legs bound. Now he threw it, alive, into the fire to cook, revolting the boys with his wanton cruelty. Judd had almost reached the end of his endurance as far as the Ringapat was concerned.

As the light of afternoon faded, dusk seemed to creep out of the earth itself, lending illusory distortions to the fallen trunks of big trees, to gnarled and writhing roots. The guardian idols towered thirty feet or more, bearing a family resemblance of gaping eye socket and painted tongue which hung derisively from a hideous mouth. Perched above the head of each one, a black predatory bird had been carved with beak bent downward and wings outspread.

"Departed ancestral heroes, I suppose," Ken suggested, "and the birds are their dark spirits. Gee, what wouldn't I give to take one of 'em back to Chicago!"

"You'll do well to take yourself back," Judd reminded him. "Forget ethnology, will you? Terii's got chow ready."

The fever warning that Judd had experienced earlier in the day now was getting the upper hand. A throbbing pulse in his throat merged with the sick pain at the back of his head, and some kind of strength seemed to be dissolving away from the pit of his stomach. He made a show of drinking the bouillon that Terii offered, but his heart began to pump violently and his knees sagged. No longer could he hide his condition from his companions. In alarm Ken forced him to down the steaming brew, built up a roaring fire, and tried to make him comfortable within the radius of its heat. The fever yielded to chills so wracking that Judd's teeth rattled like peas in a dry pod and his limbs shook uncontrollably. Lying close to the fire, he knew with a sense of dismay that, for the first time in his life, he was genuinely ill. Through a blur the looming idols seemed to advance and retreat, while the predatory birds rustled their dark wings. . . . The boy fell into a stupor that might have been sleep.

Since Sul was not to be trusted Terii stood guard while Ken snatched at a few hours of uneasy rest. The Ringapat had wrapped himself in his dirty matting and disappeared into the tambu house.

Toward midnight Judd stirred, roused from his torpor. He felt rag-weak and empty, but knew that his introductory bout of fever had come to brief end. Chills and aches had vanished; he found himself ravenously hungry. Terii, he discovered, was dozing beside a burned-out fire, head nodding above his knees. The Polynesian started when Judd spoke, remorseful that sleep should have overcome him, and he set about building up the fire.

Whatever had roused Judd he could not have told. For the first low throbbing of the drum was so whisper-faint as to be almost inaudible. But some curious vibration seemed to penetrate the inner ear, some ancient, ancestral warning—for it brought Ken out of sleep, bolt upright. And the three boys found themselves listening with strained intensity to a sound that struck the entrails rather than the ear.

"Is it what I think it is?" Ken whispered.

"If we didn't all hear it," Judd returned, "I'd say we imagined it. It's as if you could *feel* sound!"

The low throb came as a part of the orchestration of the jungle—the beat of wings, the thud of soft-padded footfall, the mysterious sibilant whispers of wary wild things—and it faded as imperceptibly as it had appeared.

A heavy, expectant silence now enveloped the village, and the boys waited with taut expectancy for the first flaw in it. Far off to the southeast other drums began to speak, and, the waiting over, they could draw breath again and cover their apprehension with a casual word.

"Calling all stations," Ken murmured. "Come in, W.C.T.U. . . ."

"Must be the back-talk Malloy told us about."

Into the east the sound shifted, more personalized now: interrogation and reply, statement and decision—a rhythmic message that invoked an image of a menacing and overwhelming power. The timbered hills were speaking; the earth answered; the sky held its breath.

"The island grapevine, sending out invitations to the feast," Ken suggested. "You can't win!"

"What do you suppose they *are* talking about?" Judd wondered. "Sul ought to know; he's one of 'em."

"Let's ask him."

But Sul was not to be found inside the tambu house.

Thoroughly aroused, the three boys made a house-to-house search of the village. But the Ringapat was not there. Like the other inhabitants of this ghostly village, their guide had vanished.

Not until dawn, however, as they hastened to break camp, did they discover that Judd's compass had disappeared with the treacherous Ringapat.

"But how in heck could he have stolen it," Ken objected, "when you practically used the darned thing for a pillow?"

"Don't ask me how," Judd snapped, "but it's gone."

Overcome with remorse, Terii held his head in his big hands. "It is my fault, Americans. While I slept, the black one stole it. *Aué te aué!*"

They sought to reassure him, but the Polynesian remained abject. His had been the responsibility of guarding camp, and he had dozed. Terii could only shake his head inconsolably.

"What do you suppose he wanted a compass for?" Ken asked. "He couldn't read it."

"He'll wear it for a nose plug most likely."

"Well—what shall we do now? Head back for Malloy's?"

"Not on your life!" Judd cried. "We've come this far and we'll keep going."

Ken grinned. "What are we waiting for, Skipper? Let's go!"

Despite the loss of the compass, the boys breathed more easily as they put behind them the ghost-ridden village of the Ringapats. By the saner light of day Sul's disappearance seemed almost in the nature of a blessing. A rising sun, hot and red, dispelled the mists of fear. Even the unknown territory of the Langalis, through which they must make their way, was less forbidding in anticipation than the actuality they were leaving behind.

Hour after hour the boys fought their way ahead, pausing only to get their bearings. Before long they began to find in the jungle signs of human passage—footprints, trees felled by stone adzes, a bridge of cane across a gorge. And their breathing quickened with the realization that the country of the dread Langalis was looming near.

Toward late afternoon they came to a break in the forest, leading them to a high bluff. Looking eagerly southward, they stood spellbound before an outflung panorama of wild and lonely splendor. Below them lay the grasslands of a superb valley, through which a river wound like some monstrous legendary reptile, its head flat as a python's, it's body sinuous and yellow-green. Great cliffs of limestone walled in the valley on three sides, while the river escaped through a deep-cleft gorge to the southeast. Through that gorge, somehow, they too must escape. . . .

Innumerable houses of bamboo and thatch clustered throughout the great valley, and patches of cultivation were arranged in terraces, skillfully irrigated.

"Aué!" Terii gasped. "The Langalis are many as grains of the sand. What if they be bad-tempered? What then, Americans?"

"So what?" Ken retorted cockily. "There's three of us, aren't there?"

Judd said quietly: "Let's go, mates!" And he led the way down a trail that twisted across the face of the limestone bluff.

CHAPTER XI Dark River

THE ENCIRCLING RAMPARTS towered against the sky, as if they would imprison forever these three aliens within their ancient stronghold. Descending to valley level, the sun's alchemy transmuted limestone into gold, vegetation into emerald, through which a thread of river flowed and was lost in silence. It was stranger than a legend. And, gazing upon it, the boys became aware of an imminence that impended, that brooded, new to their experience, half perceived and troublous. Escape now was out of the question. They could only move ahead into those imprisoning, fabulous walls of gold.

"Friendly or not," Ken muttered, striving to cast off a sense of gloomy foreboding, "these Langalis are cuts above the Ringapats, as far as intelligence goes. Look at the way they've developed this valley—those terraces and cultivations."

Here, indeed, was a system of husbandry utterly superior to the haphazard planting of the Ringapats. Timber split by stone adzes, substantial bamboo houses with hedges of croton, terraced gardens, vast numbers of pigs properly penned—all filled the boys with admiration and wonder.

"It's not like anything I've ever read or heard about the Solomon Islands," Judd marveled. "More like a valley of the moon."

"There are probably dozens of tribes like this on Guadalcanal," Ken returned, "that no one's ever seen or dreamed existed. No wonder the Ringapats are scared of these guys."

"Do you suppose this valley has never been reported to the outside world?"

"Malloy said that the few whites who'd been here hadn't come back to talk about it," the other reminded him.

"So he did! The heart of this country has never been touched."

For how many centuries, walled off from the civilized world, had the Langalis lived within this valley, cultivating their terraces, carrying on their traditions, slaying the enemies within their gates? Such a speculation served only to enhance the incalculable mystery of these Pacific hinterlands. In these remote island fastnesses the world's final "dark continent" awaited the discovery of scientists, the exploitation of world powers. Gold, iron, copper, oil, precious stones—what vast stores might lie buried in mountain, river, and gorge! The far-flung chain of the Solomons, New Hebrides, New Guinea—how much longer would they be allowed to guard from the greedy eyes of men their rich dark secrets?

Something of this wonder echoed in Judd's tone as he murmured, "Gee, Ken, these people must have been here cultivating these fields when Nero was fiddling in Rome. . . . And we're among the few who've seen it."

"Look at their irrigation system; and the way they bury their dead on those exposed platforms!" Ken's voice was quick with excitement, his eyes alight. "Lord, what an experience—the chance to see all this!"

"Yes," the other threw in quickly, "and just take a look at the Langalis themselves!"

At these words Ken snapped back to the pressure of reality. "Boy, here they come! Hold everything——"

For already the savages, if such they could be called, had discovered the presence of strangers in their valley. Three powerfully built men, almost naked, appeared not fifty yards away. They snapped to a halt, examined the boys uncertainly. Their skin was less black than that of the pygmies or the Ringapats, with a hint of Polynesian copper in its tinge. Their features too seemed less brutish and anthropoid. But their eyes were wild enough, and the men carried themselves with a reckless arrogance, a swing of unfettered movement. Battle-axes of green stone were thrust through their belts and they carried palmwood bows and arrows. They stood waiting for the strangers to declare themselves or to commit some overt act which could provoke attack.

Judd raised one hand in a gesture of good will, calling at the same moment: "Friend! Friend!"

But at sound of the boy's voice the three savages vanished as suddenly as if they'd been marionettes jerked from the stage by wires. And with their disappearance an instantaneous stillness settled upon the entire valley, as if it held its breath with waiting. No barking dogs, no crying children. Nor was there any further glimpse of man or woman. Only this ominous silence, charged with high tension.

"Maybe they're going to pull a fade-out, like the Ringapats," Ken suggested hopefully.

"Don't count on it! I'll bet there're five hundred pairs of eyes trained on us right this minute."

Reluctantly the other agreed. "I'll bet they're saying, 'Who'll have a slice of the white meat, and who prefers dark?' Well, Skipper, we're in for it! What do we do next?"

Judd answered this question by slipping the rucksack off his shoulders. "We'll sit tight and let 'em come to us. We've got to camp somewhere, and this is an open spot. At least they can't take us by surprise."

At that second a curious sound of yodeling came to

their ears. It was caught up instantly by other voices and passed along the valley. Like different instruments in an orchestra, the voices caught at a single theme, tossed it into the ether, and sent the message on its way.

"The Langali broadcasting system," Ken exclaimed. "No drums, no gong language here. This darned place is nothing but surprises."

"I could do without 'em myself."

Not unpleasant to the ear, the yodeling possessed a ventriloquial quality of great carrying power, while the valley's limestone walls became sounding boards against which the tones vibrated and expanded. There was no doubt that the presence of three strangers was being broadcast the length of Langali territory.

"Aiá!" Terii muttered, casting an apprehensive look over his shoulder. "That is no sound of men! That voice is the Varua Ino who preys upon the souls of the dead. I do not like the noises of this land!"

"I'll bet people a mile away know the color of our eyes already," Ken tried to joke, "and how many buttons I've got on my shirt."

But the thought that their presence was known the length of the valley was disquieting, and with nervous haste the boys set up the tent fly while Terii built a fire of twigs. Judd had the feeling that before dark curiosity would overcome the Langalis' caution; in the meantime there was nothing to do but sit tight and wait. And, though he didn't voice this thought, he was equally certain that he and his companions would never be allowed to leave this valley unchallenged. What strategy must be employed, what subterfuge resorted to, could be dictated only by events themselves.

Just before dark enclosed the valley a throng of men could be seen approaching—all splendid specimens of Langali manhood. In G strings and feathered topknots, some wore in addition necklaces of hornbill or dogs' teeth. All boasted nose plugs which ranged the scale from pigs' tails to bird quills.

"At least they've left their battle-axes home this time!" A note of relief echoed in Ken's words.

"But they look as if they were up to no good," the other returned dubiously.

The Langalis slowed pace as they came closer, and again Judd called out: "Friend!" then pointed to Ken, to Terii, reiterating the word.

But the expression on the faces of these reckless, splendid savages underwent no change. Neither belligerent nor friendly, it was, rather, fiercely noncommittal. Ten yards away they stood at vigilant ease, their restless black eyes raking every detail of the boys' equipment and person. Forcing a smile, Judd sought to engage them in pidgin; but if the Langalis had knowledge of this hybrid tongue they refused to employ it and maintained stubborn silence.

"The art of conversation seems to be on the decline," Ken murmured. "I have an idea that their actions speak louder than words!"

"Shouldn't wonder. I'd feel better if they'd let out a good 'Ugh!' "

At this point a new arrival shouldered his way through the throng—a fine figure of a man, somewhat darker of skin than his fellows and more magnificently ornamented.

Here, Judd felt, was a chief or sorcerer of some rank, for the younger men made way for him with deference.

"What man is this?" Terii demanded scornfully. "Why has he sent the younger men to meet us before he dares to come himself? Is he then a coward?"

"He doesn't look exactly craven," Ken muttered. "And get a load of the doorknob he's wearing!"

It was a fact that this splendid savage wore about his neck a china doorknob—the only sign of European contact the boys had yet discovered among the Langalis. The sorcerer, if such he was, carried a spear whose head had been carved from a human thighbone, so cruelly barbed that a wound from it would almost certainly prove fatal. Halting directly in front of Judd, the new-comer flung up his head with an interrogative jerk, as if demanding to know whence these intruders had come. Judd pointed to the northwest, beyond the encircling mountains—the direction of Ringapat territory. A quick, portentous murmur swept the Langalis, while a look of incredulity stamped their faces with disbelief.

The sorcerer made an explosive sound of scorn, threw some sharp unintelligible retort into Judd's face.

"He's calling me a liar," the boy muttered uneasily.

"Maybe he thinks we're friendly with the Ringapats," Ken suggested.

"I never thought of that. . . ."

Taking fire from their leader, the other Langalis burst into hooting derision. The sorcerer's right hand tightened on the shaft of his spear. He shot the strangers a look of crafty guile, and the intention behind that sloping brow was not difficult to read. Here was a moment demanding instant decision, and Judd rose to it. He flipped off the safety of the .45, instructed Ken to throw two sticks into the air.

As the pieces of wood went soaring over the head of the savage Judd shattered each piece with a single shot. Immediately the Langalis broke rank and sprang back. The sorcerer, however, managed to stand his ground, but the expression on his face was almost ludicrous in its simple range from surprise to consternation.

With a show of unconcern, as one accustomed to dealing with trifles, Judd slipped the .45 into the holster, deliberately turned his back on the sorcerer. But to Ken he muttered in aside: "The old boy's on the spot now. He's got to produce something or lose face. Don't take your eyes off him!"

With a shout of anger the sorcerer made motions to indicate that the strangers must leave the valley at once, by the same route they had come.

Stubbornly Judd refused. Instead he motioned toward the river where it flowed out through the valley and disappeared into the gorge; and his gestures left no doubt in the minds of the Langalis that he would not comply with their demand. A hum of speculation rippled through the savages, going up an angry scale. The sorcerer's fingers again tightened on the spear; but as Judd's hand leaped to the holster the man drew back. Then, mustering such dignity as remained, the sorcerer shouldered his way furiously through his followers. One by one, muttering in low guttural and with many a black look, the Langalis followed their leader.

The boys were left alone at the fire. It was a full minute before they could realize that the immediate danger had passed, and a flooding sense of relief left them voluble and unsteady.

"*Phew!*" Ken drew a hand across his forehead, cold with sweat. "You won the first round, Skipper. But getting out of this valley before the nine count, with our heads on—that's going to be another story."

"We're all right unless they jump us at close range," Judd answered, striving to conceal his genuine concern. "I haven't seen a gun in the lot, and that gives us the edge. But that sorcerer has got to deliver the goods to his men or look for another job! He'll be planning some kind of surprise for breakfast or I miss my guess."

"Do you realize we haven't seen any women or children yet?" Ken queried. "Not even any old people. Just the fighting men."

Grimly the other nodded. "I seem to remember it's the custom for women to prepare the victim for cooking!"

"H'mmm . . . They're probably busy sharpening up the knives."

That night there was little sleep. Fires were burning throughout the village; by their glow, shadowy figures came and went while the yodeling was again taken up: a hundred throats broadcasting a message of ominous intent that swelled and was answered, ricocheting from wall to wall of the imprisoned valley, causing Terii to mutter darkly of the Varua Ino and hug closer to the fire.

Breakfast was only a memory of last night's supper. Speed was more essential than food. As the boys hurriedly broke camp the sky behind the eastern mountains had scarcely paled. But by the time they had reached the flat lands leading to the river the sun had already illumined the western ramparts of the valley. And now, for the first time, women could be seen at work among the yam patches; children were herding pigs; dogs were barking—and these signs of normal village life restored some measure of the boys' flagging confidence. But some distance away two men appeared suddenly and motioned the boys to turn back. Obviously a night's sleep had not changed the Langalis' determination: the strangers should not cross their country and escape by the gorge to the south. As the boys paused, uncertain, the men began to gesticulate furiously.

"What'll we do, Skipper?"

"What can we do, except see it through?"

"Okay, let's keep moving. And we'll lick the first guy who says we can't!" Ken's cheery whistle belied the fact that his face had gone pale beneath its tan. Terii was silent and alert, carrying his bush knife in such fashion that it could be put to instant use. Judd felt taut in every nerve, keyed to a pitch of anticipation, as straight into the valley's heart they held their course, past the stilted houses, the splendid cultivations. Swarms of dogs snarled at their heels; from shadowy doorways women peered forth with bright, malicious eyes. Hostility charged the air like some intolerable current, an almost palpable force of destruction. But as yet there was no sign of the disgruntled sorcerer or his warriors.

"I'd be willing to bet we're walking straight into a trap," Ken ventured.

"Could be," the other returned, plodding stubbornly ahead. "You scared?"

"Sure I'm scared! How about you?"

"I'll say. . . ."

Warily the three boys moved toward the dark, swift-flowing river, at a point where they had seen a suspension bridge of cane. High sirio grass covered the opposite bank, a natural ambush, beyond which the limestone walls rose sheer for a thousand feet. As they advanced cautiously, every sense on the alert, a score of Langalis came to meet them—unarmed and affecting a friendly eagerness for the boys to be away and on their journey. Invitingly the savages motioned toward the bridge, yet made no attempt to lead the way. They seemed childishly anxious to persuade the strangers that they themselves had undergone a change of heart and now could be considered friends, a manner ludicrously opposed to that of the preceding evening.

At that moment Terii sounded warning. "American, armed men are across the river—in the high grass!"

The Polynesian's keen eyes had detected grass moving against the wind, the points of many spears. Something must be done and fast. Judd singled out a savage in the forefront of the Langalis, imperiously motioned him to lead the way across the bridge, straight into the waiting spears of his own people. But with a derisive laugh the man refused, spat on the earth.

Judd's .45 sent a bullet into the ground, not six inches from the savage's foot. With a howl of surprise the Langali leaped straight into the air. And before Judd could fire a second shot the man had bolted for the bridge, scurrying across with his mates at his heels.

As the last Langali reached the opposite bank the three boys followed. There they knew that the sorcerer and his men, fully armed, would be waiting for them. And even as Judd stepped foot on the grassy bank, the sorcerer himself broke cover, spear in hand. Death hung suspended in the hot sunlight. But for the moment the man offered no aggressive act; instead he motioned for the boys to retreat in the direction whence they'd come. But again Judd obdurately refused, realizing even as he did so that he was forcing the sorcerer's hand, that the man must attack now or forever lose face with his tribe.

The boy saw his antagonist's powerful arm sweep back, the spearhead glisten. At that same split second Judd fired—the luckiest shot of his life. The bullet hit the spearhead squarely, flung splinters of bone into the savage's face. Simultaneously Ken fired over the ranks of the warriors, who, as their chief was disarmed, fell back in confusion.

But it was only a momentary advantage. Not for long could this determined force be held in check. Two automatic pistols and one bush knife were no match for the darts and arrows, the battle-axes of a hundred enraged warriors. And a sickening sense of defeat struck at Judd's heart. What an end, to die like this, with his back to the wall. . . . Quickly the boy got hold of himself, motioned to his companions to drop flat in the grass. Not a moment too soon. For the first arrow went whizzing above their heads, to shatter against the limestone wall. Then the air was filled with arrows, like a whir of rain. The boys hugged the ground, shooting blindly into the waving grass. With bloodcurdling shrieks the Langalis spread out fanwise, began inevitably to close in. The air was a bedlam of sound and fury—a monstrous din that struck terror into the boys' souls. All the demons of hell seemed to have been let loose in a holocaust of destruction. Escape was impossible, annihilation but a matter of seconds.

In a flash of inspiration Judd remembered the rockets that Red Malloy had given him. Here was the last desperate chance. . . . With shaky hands the boy ripped open the rucksack, muttering to Ken: "Hold 'em off if you can, while I light this."

The cigarette lighter flared, the fuse hissed. A blazing ball of red fire arced upward from the rocket's end. Midway above the heads of the Langalis it exploded into snapping crackling torpedoes, followed by bursts of spark and flame.

In the consternation that followed there was one second of utter silence. Up went the second rocket—this one filled with torpedoes that shrieked and sizzled. Then with howls of terror the Langalis broke formation, scrambled madly for the cane bridge. The sorcerer himself was in the lead. It seemed that they could not gain the opposite bank quickly enough. They surged, shoved, clambered over their fellows. Some lost footing on the wildly swaying bridge and plunged headlong into the river.

Quick to take advantage of the enemy's rout, the boys raced along the trail under the looming walls of limestone. If only they could make that gorge at the far end, they felt certain that they would be safe. On the opposite bank the Langalis had halted and could be seen huddled in precarious conference. They must have persuaded themselves that these strangers from beyond the mountains possessed a magic better left unchallenged, for it was soon apparent that they had no intention of giving pursuit. The three boys, fleeing for their lives, knew that they had won this brush with the savages. But they dared not pause and kept on running. Once Terii stumbled, half fell to his knees. Judd saw the arrow then, deep-driven through the native's calf. He yanked it free and on they fled.

The walls of the gorge narrowed at a point where the river dropped five hundred feet over boulders and crags. The thunder of the cataract drowned the last of those hateful, yodeling cries. And with the disappearance of that dreaded sound the boys had the conviction that they had actually shaken off their enemies. What they had experienced in this strange walled valley had been like a visitation of nightmare from which, presently, they hoped to awake.

Famished, parched, haggard for sleep, they knew only the desperate urge to put as much distance as possible between themselves and the Langalis; and toward that end they drove themselves unsparingly. But Terii's wound began to slow their pace, until finally they were forced to call a halt. Already the Polynesian's leg was painfully swollen, necessitating a drastic treatment, since there was no telling with what subtle poison the barb might have been tainted.

They found themselves deep in the gorge, whose sheer clifflike walls protected them from surprise attack. Ahead, a long smooth stretch of dark river beckoned to them like a pointing arm. Here was an ideal camp site and they were all in sore need of respite.

"Tomorrow we'll start building a raft," Judd decided. "There's enough driftwood and logs, and plenty of lianas to tie 'em together. But first we'll get some food and sleep."

"And can I use 'em both!" Ken sighed, his knees buckling with exhaustion.

But though Judd understood how desperately he and his companions needed rest and nourishment, haste was almost as imperative; for their small store of supplies was rapidly dwindling, and here in the gorge there would be no natural food for their sustenance. They must reach the end of this dark river, push on as quickly as possible into the wooded plains country that led to the coast—or they would die.

Three days were consumed in constructing the raft, during which time Terii's wound took a turn for the better. The Polynesian's superb constitution, coupled with Judd's drastic doctoring, caused the painful swelling engendered by the poison to subside. It was a triumphant moment when, armed with crude flat paddles, they shoved the raft off from the river bank and climbed aboard. In the center of the platform they had erected a pole from which to suspend their rucksacks and what was left of their shoes.

Ken chuckled: "There was a time when I never wanted to see a raft again, but I swear it's my favorite means of locomotion!"

To which Judd sighed with weary satisfaction: "And I don't mind taking the weight off my own feet. How about you, Terii?"

"Ai!" came the exclamation, accompanied by an

ecstatic grin. And Terii thumped his healing wound in happy approbation.

For mile after mile the raft floated downstream, over water like dark glass, guided only by an occasional dip of a paddle. On either hand the limestone walls narrowed to unscalable heights; and once, on the edge of those cliffs, the boys made out black figures of savages gesticulating wildly. They congratulated themselves that, for the time being at least, they were beyond reach of harm.

And when, gradually, the limestone walls gave way to lesser, jungle-clad slopes, the familiar screaming of cockatoos could again be heard, the whir and swoop of bats. Here the tree python coiled himself at undulant ease, and only the slithering plash of the crocodile disturbed the smooth dark mirror of the river. As near as Judd could determine, the river at this point must be at an altitude of some four thousand feet; which meant that it would drop in a series of rapids and cascades. Every bend in the stream now became an uncertainty of suspense, since each time the boy expected to be surprised by a great drop from which they could not hope to escape in time. The accelerating current warned him that such a drop was in the offing, that soon it would be imperative to abandon the raft and strike out again on foot.

How far were they now from the coast? How long would it take them to reach Wanderer's Bay? Would they be able to win through to safety before the last of their rations had vanished, before fever or hostile arrow struck them down? These questions plagued Judd Anders day and night, giving him no rest from their insistence. The idea began to fix itself in his mind that Guadalcanal had been saving up its worst, to defeat them in the end. Seldom free from fever; shoes mildewed and rotting; guns rust-clogged and useless; bodies covered with bites of nameless insects that bored and drilled and festered—the boys knew only the blind impulse to put this repellent land behind them forever. Somewhere there must be a world of clean dry earth, of clear air, of men and women going about normal everyday concerns. But it seemed as if they themselves had been trapped eternally in this vast nihilistic smother, that they would drop unnoticed one by one, slowly to be absorbed and covered there by this patterned nothingness. . . .

When, finally, the river curved away on a western tangent and the thunder of a waterfall could be heard near at hand, they knew that they must abandon the raft and go on afoot, always striking to the southeast.

They watched their raft float away on the back of the dark river, saw it disappear around the bend to plunge to its destruction. Then, tightening their belts, the three boys struck off into a chasm that was the dry, boulder-strewn bed of a river and offered easier passage than the jungle. For the past twenty-four hours it had been raining steadily and there was a trickle of water in the chasm's bed. And here they were to have their most

terrifying experience, one that for the rest of their lives
had the power to reappear in their dreams and set them
shivering.

The chasm was some five miles long, and Judd was
concerned with the possibility of a flood overtaking
them before they should reach open country. Ken had
barely recovered from a bout of fever that left him
quickly fatigued, while climbing over the huge boulders
caused Terii's wounded leg to swell and stiffen. Though
speed was of the utmost importance, the boys' pace was
limited to that of the weakest member.

On either hand the chasm walls rose sheer and smooth,
where even a lizard would have been put to it to find a
foothold. In the absence of sunlight, the gray sheeting
rain, the dearth of birds and even insects, the place was
overwhelmingly gloomy and forbidding. Climbing
boulders, skirting ledges, the boys plodded on doggedly,
knees bent, heads bowed with growing fatigue. The
dead world through which they passed seemed greedy
to suck away their strength. It struck them silent. Too,
the sound of a voice when it came was so empty and lost
as to be almost intimidating. The wispy air of the chasm
seemed to feel for them, to fumble about their faces,
their necks, their legs, then steal past, leaving them chill
and clammy.

The rain increased steadily to a tropical deluge of
stinging power; and Judd knew then that a flood was
inevitable, that somehow they must entrench themselves above its highest level. But the only spot of any

elevation they could find came at a bend in the chasm, and with that they were forced to be content. Night was almost upon them; rumbling in the near distance, an electrical storm was working itself into a fury. Lightning lashed the sky with zigzags of white wire.

Since the cigarette lighter was long since useless, and matches had turned to pulp, the boys huddled miserably together for warmth, there on the elevated ledge. Under the dark-looming walls of the chasm they waited for the flood to come.

They hadn't long to wait. The storm struck with a rush and a roar. Thunder reverberated within the enclosing walls with ear-splitting force. Brilliant bursts of lightning revealed a rushing torrent in the chasm's bed; and with each fresh flare the water seemed to have risen a foot. Unbelievably soon it was in full flood, fighting its insensate way over boulder and ledge, adding its fury to the din of reverberation. And the boys clung together there in darkness, nearly at the end of their physical endurance, fighting down the threat of rebellious nerves.

Through tight lips Judd muttered: "I guess this is the end, mates. . . ." And his voice cut through the obscurity, tense and unnatural.

Against the compulsion of his words Terii cried out: "Why should this be? We have come far. The sea is near. Aiá! But this is all bad!"

Ken could find no words, either of agreement or

reassurance; the icy rain set his teeth chattering, and he clung to his companions, shaking uncontrollably.

Protected from the full force of the avalanche by the bend of the chasm, they could only huddle together and wait, praying for some miracle to come to their salvation. The cold breath of the water was upon them even before the water itself reached their bodies. And when Terii cried out: "The water is at my knees!" he was only voicing the common horror.

What was taking place was a catastrophe beyond human resource or courage. No escape remained unless that relentless torrent stopped rising. With every faculty and fixed gaze thrusting ahead into darkness, each boy sought to discover whether, in this place of slimy entombment, he had reached his end. Semiconscious under the desperation of sustained effort, they no longer spoke as the water reached up their thighs, passed their waists. And they drew each breath as if it might be the final act of living.

Only in that second when lightning revealed that the water was chest-high, and the next pitiless flash showed no increase, did they dare to believe that it had reached its level. But it seemed an agonizing eternity before they knew the exquisite relief of feeling that water recede—down, down, almost as rapidly as it had risen.

Two days later, nearer dead than alive, three human scarecrows descended a ridge, came to a break in the jungle which revealed a breath-taking glimpse of blue horizon. It was the ocean—the vast Pacific at last! And a cry broke from their hoarse throats as a brisk wind brought a tang of salt, the rank odor of mangroves— sweeter in this magic moment than any other smell on earth. Ragged, footsore, half starved, the boys found themselves on top of a basalt cliff, some six hundred feet above the sea.

"Where are we?" Ken gasped, sinking to his knees in exhaustion. "This can't be Wanderer's Bay——"

"At least we're free of that blasted jungle," Judd managed to answer. "What more can you want?"

"Nothing, Skipper. . . . Don't ever say 'jungle' to me again!"

At their backs the lowering peaks of Guadalcanal were shrouded in mist, as if jealously to guard their strange dark secrets; below lay a limitless expanse of blue Pacific, *their* element, Judd thought, their world.

Terii was peering cautiously over the rim of the cliff. He came to his feet at a bound; a violent shout burst from him. "Americans!" He gesticulated wildly toward the bay below. "Tell me if what I see is true!"

The others rushed to the rim, peered in the direction of Terii's outflung arm. For one second their vision, conditioned to the half-gloom of the jungle, swam in the sun. Spread like the painted depth of a stage set, the bay was spangled with points of fire. And as they gazed, scarcely daring to credit what their eyes beheld, the pits of their stomachs dissolved, became aching space.

For six hundred feet below, white against the blue, a

ship rode at anchor: a trim, two-masted square-rigger whose brightwork flashed in the sun.

And a sound divided between a gulp and a sob ripped from Judd Anders' throat: "It's—oh, Lord, it *is!* It's the *Island Queen.*"

CHAPTER XII Hull-Down for Action

HUGGING THE CLIFF, the three boys fixed their gaze as if tranced upon that gleaming splinter of wood which was a ship—*their* ship. After Judd's first involuntary exclamation no one spoke: their hearts were too full for speech. Almost landlocked, the *Island Queen* lay hidden in a deep harbor that seemed incalculably remote and secret.

They were unable to discover any sign of activity aboard the brig, nor could they distinguish a flag flying at the peak of the gaff. But one fact was certain: here was the secret harbor about which Haru Osaka had bragged. From this hidden base the *Island Queen* had been forced into ignominious service. And as this conviction fastened itself upon the boys their wills hardened with purpose. As far as eye could reach the coast line was empty of native village or white man's habitation: another evidence of Hirohito's long-range planning. This remote and unfrequented spot had been made to order for its base purpose.

Ken was the first to break silence. "This certainly isn't Wanderer's Bay, Skipper. Bill Boyd's trading station would be down there, and the ketch we're supposed to hire—instead of a Nip hangout."

Judd's teeth flashed white. "I'd rather see that ship down there than any dozen ketches!"

"You and me both, Skipper! But the next thing is to get down to the beach. Short of a parachute, it won't be so easy."

"Child's play!" Judd retorted. "Come on, you guys, let's get moving."

"A spider couldn't scale that cliff without being seen," Ken protested. "And I've a hunch we don't want to be spotted by anyone aboard the brig."

"You're right we don't. We'll find Haru Osaka aboard, unless I miss my guess; not to mention Einar Karlson——"

"But just how do you think we're going to round 'em up? The brig's been turned into an arsenal, and we haven't so much as a slingshot."

Reluctantly the other agreed. "But what are we going to do—sit here and let 'em decoy American troops?"

"Not if we can help it! Let's give our luck one more chance. It's done pretty well by us."

Judd laughed exultantly. "On our way, fellas. The best is yet to come!"

They slipped into the protective shelter of the bush, whose every leaf and liana they had come to know by heart. The trail they made was no more than a circuitous spiral of descending twists, where in some places they used lianas as ropes to swing and lower themselves. There were moments when their breath caught at the sheer hazard of their descent; and not until they reached the first solid slope of the foothills above the bay did they dare pause to reconnoiter.

They found themselves in a dense coconut grove—old trees of many years' standing; and without even waiting to slake their thirst with the nuts lying so invitingly on the ground, they shoved ahead. In a clearing, floodlighted with tropic sun, they stumbled upon another Nipponese storehouse, identical with the one they had discovered so long ago—a prefabricated building painted mustard-green and daubed with camouflage.

"The supply base for the brig!" Judd exploded. "Boy, is this a break!"

A glance through the screened window revealed case after case of supplies and ordnance.

"Just like old times," Ken chortled. "Brother, here's where we help ourselves."

Armed with automatics and plenty of ammunition, they pressed on into the grove, warily, following the trail where it widened into a well-used track that led down to the beach.

Through tapering aisles of gray palm trunks they finally caught sight of their ship. Even as they drew up, uncertain of what their next move should be, they saw that one of the smallboats, swinging in the davits, was being lowered into the water. They were close enough now to count the men who dropped overside.

"The jailbirds," Ken breathed. "What do you suppose they're up to?"

A water cask was lowered down to them and Judd replied: "There's your answer. Going ashore for water. Another break for our side!"

"Sure, if they don't come in this direction."

Straight as a ruled line, the smallboat headed toward the grove where the boys crouched in hiding. It was a ticklish moment. If a single shot were fired those aboard the brig would either weigh anchor and stand out to sea or come to the assistance of the crew ashore. And either eventuality meant disaster for the boys. Tense and trembling, they crouched low in the scrub, their eyes fixed upon that approaching smallboat.

As it neared the shore the jailbirds sprang into the shallows, dragging the boat up the beach. It could be seen that the men were fully armed with rifles and bush knives, a formidable-looking crew. The cask was passed ashore, slung on poles, then the men disappeared into the scrub, this time on a tangent that led away from the spot where the boys lay hiding.

When they had disappeared Judd came to his feet. Motioning to his companions to follow, he raced toward the beach and the smallboat. A bare hundred yards from shore the *Island Queen* lay at anchor in deep-shelving water, and there seemed to be no sign of activity about her decks. Haru Osaka and Einar Karlson must be below.

With Terii at the oars the boat swept across the intervening strip of water, slid silently up under the brig's counter. Judd's bare feet made no sound as he climbed the rope ladder and dropped on the well-remembered deck, Terii close at his heels. The boy motioned to Ken to remain at the ladder to cover their retreat, while he and Terii, with drawn guns, crept swiftly toward the companionway.

The door leading below was half open. Judd peered into the gloom, listening intently. But he could hear no sound above the wild hammering of his heart. Down the stairs he inched, scarcely daring to draw breath. The door at the far end of the corridor that led to the main cabin seemed a mile away! But somehow he reached it, and the hand that turned the knob was steady. For in this crisis Judd Anders felt cold with purpose. Through him stormed the thought of all that he and Ken and Terii had suffered at the hands of these men; and he thought of Conk—who ought still to be alive. His brain was like a deep cold spring. He knew what he must do. . . .

But whom would he find in that cabin? Karlson or

Osaka? Perhaps both. . . . Silently the door swung open.

In what once had been Judd's bunk Einar Karlson lay asleep. The boy's glance swept the room. No one else was there; and a grim smile flicked Judd Anders' lips as slowly he raised his gun, drew deliberate aim on a knothole in the bulkhead, a foot above the head of the sleeping German. The detonation of the shot was deafening.

Instantly Einar Karlson was on his feet. One hand reached for the gun under his pillow. But Terii was ahead of him. With a movement quick as the striking of a snake the Polynesian lunged forward. The weight of his body bore the German to the floor. Caught within that relentless grip, Einar Karlson was powerless. His eyes blazed with impotent fury as he struggled against Terii's steellike arms.

"Sorry to have interrupted your nap, Herr Karlson" —Judd grinned—"but you'll have plenty time to catch up with sleep where you're going."

Einar Karlson must have been an excellent insurance risk, for he neither paled nor trembled. After the first flash of recognition his eyes hardened and slitted, his mouth drew back from his teeth in a sneer. "The smart young Americans," he said scornfully. "*Donnerwetter,* how long do you think you will get away with this?"

"Where's Osaka?" the boy shot back at him.

"*Ach!* But wouldn't you like to know," the German jeered.

"You'll tell us before we get through, my friend!"

"If you believe that you are a bigger *dummkopf* than I thought."

Terii was tearing a sheet into strips. "Shall I bind him, American?" he demanded.

Judd assented. "And a gag will help to keep him quiet, since he doesn't want to talk."

Leaving Einar Karlson helpless for the moment, the boys set out to look for Haru Osaka. Familiar as Judd was with every possible hiding place, they searched the brig from truck to keel. But there was no sign of the little Japanese.

"Maybe he just wasn't aboard this trip," Ken suggested.

"He's somewhere handy, and you can lay to that," the other retorted. "It wouldn't surprise me to see him materialize out of thin air."

"Listen, Skipper," the other went on, a note of anxiety in his voice. "We've got to move fast. The jailbirds must have heard that shot. They've got rifles, and the brig's in easy range——"

"Right you are. A bird in the hand's worth two in the bush. We've bagged Karlson. With enough rope Osaka will hang himself. It's mainsail haul, my lad, for Australia! Let's get going!"

Ken gaped. "You think the three of us can manage the brig?"

"With good luck and fair weather, sure!"

Ken burst into a laugh. "Then what are we waiting for?"

A sudden sharp exclamation from Terii interrupted them. The native was staring toward the open water beyond the reef. Following the direction of his gaze, they saw what, for a moment, looked like the varnished back of a whale heaving to the surface. It was a giant submarine. And without further evidence than the periscope they knew instantly that it was the same sub they had encountered once before.

They bolted for the companionway, raced toward the main cabin. There Einar Karlson was struggling futilely against his bonds. Judd shoved the barrel of the .45 against the German's skull. There was no compunction in the boy now: he felt cold with unshakable resolve. This man was his country's enemy.

"Listen, Karlson. Speak fast and tell the truth if you can. Is Osaka aboard that sub?"

The pale eyes glittered, seeking to determine behind Judd Anders' resolute face the length to which the boy actually would go. Was he bluffing? Sweat started on the German's forehead; a look very like fear flickered at the back of his eyes. He swallowed convulsively against the gag. Then slowly the man nodded his head in affirmative.

"I thought so!" Judd snapped. "Now listen again. I'm untying you. You're going to walk out on deck as if nothing had happened. But I'll have you covered from the second you step through that door. One false move and I'll let you have it, understand?"

Again the German nodded.

"Good!" the boy ground out. "You'll stand beside this porthole, and you'll signal the sub to come alongside. Savvy?"

Again the pale eyes flickered, the head nodded assent.

"Okay, Karlson. I guess we understand each other. But if you want to die, remember I'm right here to help you!" And with those words of warning Judd ripped the gag out of the German's mouth, while Terii cut loose the bonds.

Einar Karlson came to his feet, flexing his muscles, and his eyes traveled from the barrel of the automatic to Judd's eyes. The man's mouth twisted. "I understand, Herr Kapitan," the erstwhile first mate muttered. "I value my own life more than Osaka's. I will do what you say."

"Get out there then! And remember, this gun will be six inches from your spine, and I'm a good shot. . . ."

The plan in Judd's mind, so hastily conceived, was now fully formed. He knew that he was taking a long chance, but there was no alternative.

Karlson stepped through the door leading to the deck, while Ken crouched at the porthole to cover him. Judd handed his own gun to Terii and motioned the native to take a place on the opposite side of the porthole. Karlson was playing ball, for with one arm the German was making motions for the sub to come alongside.

Judd raced across the cabin. His fingers trembled as he worked at the secret panel in the bulkhead. The spring clicked. The panel slid back. Into the opening Judd thrust his hand. *The dynamite was still there.*

As the boy cut the fuse his heart was hammering with great violent strokes against his breastbone. That fuse had to be exactly right. . . .

The submarine, fully surfaced now, was swinging in a circle to come alongside the brig. The boy saw that her conning-tower hatch was wide open, and a wild elation swept through him. He saw, too, a stocky little figure, immaculate in white, emerge from the conning hatch.

Across the narrowing strip of water Haru Osaka hailed his confederate. The little Oriental's voice was as silky as ever, but the words he spoke issued in the accent of command. "A large American convoy is sixty miles northeast of here," he called. "You will weigh anchor at once, Karlson—intercept the convoy and fly your signal of distress as usual. I will do the rest!"

Even as Einar Karlson mumbled the words of assent Judd Anders struck the match. There came the hissing sputter of the fuse. The stick of dynamite sailed through the porthole. Timed to perfection, it curved through the air, passed neatly into the sub's open hatch.

The Japanese never knew what hit them. The explosion was immediate. With a thunderous detonation the giant submarine split apart. Flame and smoke shot upward. The *Island Queen* recoiled, rolled her rails under as a rain of splintered wood and metal struck her decks like hail. The boys were flung to the floor; but the stout little ship righted herself, rocking violently upon the agitated waters.

Einar Karlson picked himself up out of the scuppers, half dazed from a blow on the head. His mouth sagged foolishly; and in this moment he was a far cry from the hard and competent seaman of former days. Of the submarine and Haru Osaka not a trace remained, only an oily slick upon the water and pieces of shattered debris. Already the gray, sinister shapes of sharks were closing in. . . .

It was only a matter of minutes before Karlson was again bound hand and foot, locked into a cabin with the port nailed shut. And scarcely had this been accomplished when the jailbirds, attracted by the explosion, broke from the jungle and dashed to the beach. In vain they searched for the smallboat.

As Judd barked the command, "Mains'l haul!" and canvas spilled from the yards, a volley of shot ripped out from shore, while shouts and curses turned the air blue. But already the *Island Queen* was swinging to her anchor, presenting only her stern to the rifles. Terii and Ken, aloft, shook the main-tops'l from its harbor gaskets and the land breeze came to the brig's salvation. Canvas swelled drum-taut. With anchor apeak and Judd Anders at the helm, the brig gathered way, swept through the passage in the reef—out into the open Pacific.

One backward glance toward shore revealed a huddle

of men standing helplessly in the shallows, staring after the vanishing brig.

"Maybe the crocodiles will get 'em!" Ken shouted from aloft.

To which the boy at the wheel yelled back: "Even a croc draws the line somewhere!"

The breeze freshened smartly and the *Island Queen* raced before it, fleet as a gull; while at her back the somber broken peaks of Guadalcanal diminished in size, grew dim and mysterious with distance, were swallowed by the sea. . . .

Five days later, a hundred miles off the coast of Australia, Judd Anders sighted a smudge on the horizon— the smoke of a ship appearing in the distance. Through his binoculars he presently made out the superstructure of the ship itself rising over the curve of ocean.

A whistle escaped the boy. "An American destroyer, by the look of her!" he exclaimed. "One of those new single-stackers. And bearing straight down on us!"

The destroyer's flag was soon clearly visible: red, white, and blue against the sky. But as the ship bore down closer the boys could see that all her guns were trained upon the *Island Queen*. Since the brig was flying the American flag at the peak of her gaff there seemed to be no reason for this hostile action.

Presently the destroyer signaled for the brig to heave to. When Judd had complied with this request a motor launch put smartly out over the waves, covered by the destroyer's unswerving guns. The three boys, standing bewildered at the rail, could see white-jacketed sailors armed with rifles, and a machine gun mounted on the launch's bow. In the stern sheets a snappy-looking officer scanned the brig through glasses.

The launch swept alongside and the officer scrambled up the ladder. His eyes were sharp and brightly blue in a tanned face, and the gaze that swept the brig's deck was quick and businesslike. "Where's the Jap?" the officer barked out.

"If you mean Haru Osaka——" Judd began.

"That's who I mean!" the other snapped back at him. "We know all about this Q-boat. And what's your part in this?"

To Judd it was all instantly clear. But it took a full half hour in the main cabin, where the ship's papers and commission from the New Zealand Government were still in the secret compartment, and the final conclusive evidence of Einar Karlson himself, to convince the young lieutenant that the boys were on the square and that Haru Osaka had been well taken care of.

"As long as I can't get Osaka I'll settle for Karlson." The young officer grinned. "He heads the enemy agent lists from London to New York to Melbourne. If you were in the service, my lads, you'd probably get a citation for the job you've done."

"To heck with the citation," Judd came back at him, smiling. "All we ask is to be able to join up. Any Marines in Australia yet?"

"They're on their way, young fella. We're going to make it hot for Tojo. But," he added as an afterthought, "you'll need a few square meals before they'll sign you on. The three of you look like a haul of June shad."

Terii broke in to exclaim: "Sir, Samoan is American too! I be Marine, no?"

The lieutenant threw back his head and laughed. "Business is picking up. Well, my lads—anything you need, before I escort you to Cairns?"

"We could use a few more hands in the rigging," Judd suggested.

"Easy enough. Anything else?"

"You bet! I'd like to get Herr Einar Karlson off this ship," the boy cried.

The lieutenant's mouth was grim as he cast a look at the German. Karlson was making a fine show of indifference, a sneer twisting his lips; but his arrogance was a shell of his former manner. He had reached the end of his road and he knew it. A pair of husky sailors hustled him rudely toward the rope ladder.

As the motor launch put back smartly over the waves toward the waiting destroyer, the young lieutenant turned to salute three boys, standing shoulder to shoulder at the brig's rail. "Happy hunting, you guys!" the officer called.

Clear and sure their answer returned: "Happy hunting, yourself!"